Ghostly Tales for Christmas Eve

CROWVUS

All stories are the property of their authors. To preserve the
authors' unique voice, stories are unedited.

First Published in 2018
Crowvus, 53 Argyle Square, Wick, KW1 5AJ

ISBN: 978-0-9957860-6-6

www.crowvus.com

Contents

8. **Call Me Autumn**
   by Mark Gibson
   A ghost created with an artistic painting of words and imagery.
9. **I'll Wait for You**
   by Ellen Evers
   A gripping confession to the reader.
10. **The Ghost in the Mansion**
   by Daniel Metcalfe
   A malevolent ghost in a place of sanctuary.
11. **Christmas Presence**
   by Chris Palmer
   A frightening but hopeful story filled with ghostly mystery.
12. **The Light of the Christmas Star**
   by Stephen Wade
   A psychological story which haunts the reader from beginning to end.
13. **Just Your Imagination**
   by Lizzy Bayly
   An intriguing tale with a plot which keeps the reader guessing.
14. **Treworgey's Maid**
   by Ellen Morrisson
   An edgy story which skilfully combines a modern storyline and an ageless theme.

Foreword

Dear Readers,

We are almost bursting with excitement to share this anthology of brand-new ghost stories with you, just in time for Christmas 2018.

No one knows where the tradition of telling ghost stories at Christmas came from, but it is one that has endured into the modern age of internet and mobile phones. It transports us back to those days of glowing firelight and the eerie flickering of a guttering candle.

In the pages of this book, you will be transported to different parts of the world; different times; different imaginations… With each story you read, you will be joining with all those generations of people who joined in the tradition of Christmas ghost stories, and whose voices are now those whispers of the past that you may hear as the nights grow darker and the veil becomes thinner.

Wishing you a Merry Christmas and many happy hours of reading!

The Crowvus Team

Present

by Gemma Dobson

(1st Place)

She was always on time. Never a second late. Always looking at her watch. Even when she was rushing her morning breakfast bar, she would look at that thing. She was always so busy. Even when she was a child she was always on time for school. What teenager asks for an alarm clock for their birthday? Even in the crisp, white winter snow she would put her boots on and wait for the school bus that never showed up on time. That's how everyone seemed to be now, rushing, busy. Always looking at their phones. Checking their virtual lives. The life of that little blue square, more important than physical life around them. Posting about their lives on Facesnap. The lives they claimed to be sharing, whilst sat next to their partners without a word spoken. Tapping away, commenting on each other's photographs. Instead of taking the time to look at their love right beside them. Sharing breaths. Sharing paths. Love, lives, time. Everyone seems to have forgotten this.

I hated that little clock handcuffed to my Lynsey. Always beeping away. Counting her footsteps. Calling her, messaging her. That virtual space of nothing. You can't touch, feel or smell time. And what is a clock? What are those bells that ring on the hour, echoing around town telling everyone what TIME it is. Time is nothing but bothersome to keep us on time for work. On time for chores. It wakes us up, telling us we cannot be late. We can never truly be in a moment. I hated time. For me it doesn't exist now, never really did anyway. I was never one to follow it. Always late or as my husband would say to people, 'Oh she just thinks time stops.'

Every morning Lynsey headed to work in her smart grey suit and blouse. Crisply creased symmetrically down the sides, from her shoulders all the way down to her shiny black pointed boots. Like a hard flat 2D drawing. Straight black lines to perfection like an artist's sketch of a model on a catwalk. She was as pretty as a model. Strong cheekbones, long legs. Always looking very serious. I would watch her and smile but she would just sit tapping away at her phone as I told her stories from my bus travels.

I loved riding the bus, sitting with different people every day. Some familiar faces that would smile and nod at you. You would become a part of their lives and they a part of yours. I was never going anywhere. I didn't have a destination like the others. I wasn't in any rush. I just enjoyed sitting on the blue squared, worn seats. Old wrappers of food stuffed down the sides from a stranger who had been feeling peckish and enjoyed a Rocky caramel biscuit. The wrapper glowing from the dark gaps, wedged tightly between the hard-cold metal and soft, warm seat. The empty Coca-Cola bottle, that spends its day rolling up and down, being kicked around by strangers' wet shoes. All sharing and repeating a moment. Listening to conversations, sometimes joining in when welcomed. The noisy teenagers filled with hormones that you could smell after they had finished school in their P.E. kits. The toddlers whining at their mothers to look out of the window. Crying to be lifted from the pram so they could stand on the seats and watching lives pass by out of the windows, as their mothers handed them gold chocolate coins.

My husband had a car, but he always liked the radio on and I found it too distracting. I loved to see and meet new people, be in the lives of strangers. You learn so much. Wondering where they were going as they stepped off the bus in to the dark, cold evenings. Picturing them making their way home to their families, where their partners have set the dinner table. The children running around filled with energy after being so good all day in school. Scouse simmering on the cooker. Filling the cold winter air with the smells of broths stewing. Waiting to warm the bellies and hearts of the families.

Winter produces the best smells. Stews, cinnamon, citrus, pine, wood burning chimney smoke. Those Christmas smells in the air making people smile, filling them with festive cheer. I loved Christmas. I would always make my husband dress up as Father Christmas and wake Lynsey. Letting her have a sleepy, dream like peek at Santa placing presents under our tree. Taking a bite from the mince pies we had baked. Washing it down with some milk she had left out for him. The magic and excitement lighting and waking her drowsy eyes. Eddie would always have her sit and watch It's a Wonderful Life. And every year remind her that we are all like George Bailey. We are all important to each other. Over the last years she stopped watching it, though Eddie made Liam and Isla watch it, but even they had become hard to distract from their phones. I wanted to remind her of these things, remind her of life. I wanted her to see what I saw. Feel what I'd felt. Lynsey was work mad, she needed to spend more time with her children, her husband. Christmas is the most magical time to do this, but she was always too busy. Even sitting, squashed around mine and Eddie's table with the kids arguing over who won the prize from the cracker, she would still answer her ringing phone. She was never in a moment.

The school children all thought I was mad. 'Hey look. There's that crazy old lady who sits on the bus every day. She is so weird.' They would whisper and laugh. Then I would hear a polite young lady saying. 'Leave her alone. She might have dementia or something.' That was sweet of her but no, no dementia. I just enjoyed riding the bus around the town I grew up in, lived in all my life. I had watched it change over the years as more green land was torn away and replaced with ugly new houses. I didn't like the new houses. They were too modern for me, too plain. I liked a home to be a home, filled with pictures on the walls. Ours was like an art gallery. My Lynsey and Isla and Liam. Every September I would get new pictures of my two grandchildren. I would beam with pride at their new uniforms. Their forced smiles at starting back at school. And every September I had to find an empty spot on the wall or the units where I could fit the new ones. Often people would come in to our house and comment on them all. And I would smile proudly at all those memories. All those moments frozen, timeless. That captured moment controlling time, pausing it. Allowing it to live forever. Special moments, new-born. First smiles. First solid, messy foods. First steps. School. Holidays. Birthdays. Graduation. Wedding. And then all those precious memories repeated with new life, framed proudly. Not like the ones today, that Isla and Liam used to show me. Oh no! Not the ones of girls doing that strange thing, looking like goldfish when they come right to the front of the glass, staring at you, then sharing it to the world. I would watch my grandchildren holding their phones whilst having a conversation with me or rather me asking them what they had been up to and them grumbling something or other back. Conversations floating in the air. Disappearing as those electronic pings sounded. Demanding the attention and always gaining it. I would hear those bloody pings more than the birds tweeting in the morning.

Lynsey was always attached to some sort of electronic device. Even when it was in her bag she had this black plastic, shiny thing wedged around her ear. She would press a button on the side of it and just start talking to no one. And the kids called me crazy. She was always at work never off duty. I know she was a busy Lawyer but sometimes I wondered whether she was human. So, I decided to give her an early gift this Christmas Eve of her car breaking down.

I waited for her on the bus I had travelled on for many years. I wanted her to remember her life. I can't remember the last time she rode a bus. The moment she turned seventeen, she learnt to drive. Said she couldn't rely on buses to get her to places on time. I smiled and watched as she wobbled down the aisle. Grabbing on to the cream painted metal poles, as though on high adventure ropes. Swinging from one to the next. Accidentally pressing the small square red plastic button, hitting the word stop. She quickly looked back at the driver, flushed red cheeks of embarrassment as she apologised. She sat down next to the window. I smiled, a warmth inside filling me as the heat released from her cheeks, turning them back to their pale, soft pink. She looked on fondly as she began to relax.

Sometimes I sat on that bus by myself, although I was never alone. Of course, I always had the driver Dave and he was so polite I think he liked me staying on there. I kept him company, had many conversations with him, so many we even exchanged Christmas cards. I loved to rest my feet on top of the grey grids of the bus allowing the heat to travel up my legs, warming my cold body and removing them every so often when it began to burn. This was my favourite time of the year to ride the bus. Watching the children getting all excited about what Father Christmas was going to bring them. And it was such easy conversation,

'So, is Santa going to bring you some presents?' I would say to their shy little faces, and their smiles would shine through their big bright eyes. Nodding slowly and warily at a strange old lady asking them what they were hoping to receive off Jolly Old St Nicholas, and whether they had been good girls and boys. Their mothers politely engaging and smiling away proudly at their children chattering. So much so that at the end of their journeys they would smile and wish you all the best. Their little hands waving as they shouted, 'Bye' being carried off the bus, filled with excitement. It's such a shame how a child becomes so disengaged from a world they were once so engaged with, but here was Lynsey sat re-engaging with that world. Memories awakening of our Christmases.

This time of year, the bus was always filled with shoppers all excited on their way to buying gifts for loved ones. And the stressed-out parents rushing to get that next fishing game, Cod before it sold out. Over the years I watched the bus get quieter as more people bought their gifts from their phones. It was a quiet morning today with just myself, the driver Dave and Lynsey, still attached to that weird shiny black thing. It looked like some sort of bug nested around her ear. She stared out of the window her smile faded. Her damp head resting against the cold wet window, seemingly lost, sad. Jerking along as the bus drove over the speed bumps. Her head knocking in to the glass. I wanted to take her hand and tell her how much I loved her and that I would always be with her. I wanted to be able to talk with her just one last time. I wanted her to release the pain she was feeling. I used to be able to help with that. I got up from my seat and wobbled my way along to her. I stood beside her and watched her for a moment, smiling fondly, then sat next to her and took in her beautiful scent of sweet, fresh flowers. She always smelt so beautiful. I sat next to her rubbing my faded cold hands, squeezing them in between my beige netted legs. She looked over her shoulder at me and it was as though there was a slight smile on her face just for a moment, as though she had seen me. A warm smile. A smile of reminiscence, but then she looked back out of the window and her eyes began to shimmer. Filling and rising until a warm tear fell down her soft, cold pink cheek. And more came and fell like the condensation dripping down the glass. Each drop holding a memory forming in to pools, like the puddles on the roads, reflecting like an old movie with ripples rewinding. Each tear, each drop holding a story. She wiped the tears with my handkerchief. I wanted to wrap my arms around her and hold her tightly, just as I did when she was born, tell her everything was going to be okay. Take in her scent from her auburn hair that shone like the leaves on a glowing autumn day.

She shook her head, wiped her tears and removed the slug like plastic from her ear, the removed her beeping, black watch. She let time slip away. She was in her moment, her emotions, her memories. Just as I wished. She watched the couple that got on the bus that day. The man wrapping his arm around his partner, his love, his life. Lynsey had slipped away from Dan. I could tell she missed those moments with him. She had told me once, she wondered whether her and Dan would be as close as me and her father were. I always told her she needed to be at home when she was at home. Let everything else go. She needed to see the children get on the bus with their parents happily shrieking Jingle Bells repeatedly just as Liam and Isla, my beautiful grandchildren did when they were younger. Talking of how excited they were about the presents they had wished for. She needed reminding of the warm Christmas smells that blew in through the open doors as they hissed open. The apples and cinnamon melting away at the red wax, spreading its scents across the bright twinkling streets. She needed to see the houses glowing, sparkling, singing and dancing. Illuminating the streets. Warming the dark, cold early nights. She needed reminding of all presence and absence to become present in her life and her loved ones.

I softly placed my old wrinkled hand on top of hers. I couldn't feel her delicate warm hand anymore, but she felt something as she smiled and wiped away her teary eyes that glistened like the lights on the tree shining on to the silver tinsel. We sat watching the world go by as the turquoise and cream bus filled with strangers' conversations. All of them sharing time and journeys to their homes, their lives.

The bright white, long strip lights flickered on as the early night drew in. She stood from that old warm seat, the seat I had sat on for many years. Where many stories had been collected and stored, padding it. Where time never existed and moments were soaked up in the sponges. Memories remaining forever. She smiled warmly looking back at the bus now empty as people made their way back to their warm houses. Where they wrapped up their gifts and each other. All letting time go, being in their present and nothing else. She made her way to the front of the bus where she exchanged festive wishes with Dave who spoke so fondly of me. He showed her all the Christmas cards I had given him over the years. I secretly had a little crush on Dave. He always got an extra kiss at the end of his card. He put them on display every year in his second little home. She then stepped off graciously still holding my old initial, stitched handkerchief that she had made at school for me one Christmas, and wiped her cold, wet pink nose, watching the bus drive away from my home, my life. I smiled affectionately as I watched Dan, Eddie and the kids walk down the pathway to my forever delightful little girl returning home.

Always be in the moment.

The Globe

by Isabelle Mills

(Children's Winner)

I exhale with a sigh, a wisp of smoke curling out ahead of me like the perfumes of a sweet, oaken fire. Dissipating into the air with one sweep of someone's tartan scarf, my breath is hushed like a festive secret, crackling the air with exhilarating mystery. My fingers are laced with a frost of prolonged exposure, parchment paper-yellow at the tips where I grip my weathered list. Pride flutters in my chest as I tick each line of swirling writing off with a nod of satisfaction. Leather gloves, a stash of rich, salted fudge, a coveted book collection for my little brother, and… still a gift left to buy for my sister, Anne. Peering up from my secluded spot under the overhanging post office roof, my eyes follow the scattered snowfall of shoppers whispering and hurrying through the road, their thick boots unwrapping the delicate layers of snow to unveil the cobbled ground. The village clock chimes four o'clock, and the waft of honey parsnips and roasted chestnuts from the chimneys indicate that it is nearly the end of the day. I scurry across the square, my footprints erasing behind me like the tracks of a woodland animal, as I slip into a cluster of shopping chalets.

Fairy lights cast a soft glow over the timber, but my heart dips as I realise the Christmas Eve visitors have nearly stripped the place bare. Some chalets are boarded up, signs for Christmas trees and chutney ready to be taken down over the coming days, the drinks stall straining to be able to fill three quarters of my mug with steaming hot chocolate. Panic creeps into my thoughts; how awful it would be if I found nothing for Anne! A faint lullaby of music sings gently like a lone carol singer in the distance. At the end of the row, one chalet roars like a bonfire. "Christmas Eve special!" a large man cheers, "half price for any of my unique, hand-crafted snow globes!" Marvelling at the cluttered shelves of gold and ruby paint, all intricately moulded with detailing and charm, I let myself be lured in to the grotto. "Searching for anything in particular?" he beams, pink lights flashing from his holly-green jumper. Then I notice it- the copper-gilded snow globe- absent of elves or reindeer or candy canes, but instead featuring a solitary girl, knelt before a rustic doorway in the snow. The figurine child has a gentle, quiet expression, as if she might be singing or praying.

"There is no music in that one," the man cocks his head thoughtfully, "but it still lights up a room." With a simple twist, the candle beside the figurine on the doorstep illuminates, and snowflakes begin to drift around the scene.

I hand over the money to the man in a daze. How kind of me, I can't help gleefully reflecting as I cross the square.

How happy Anne will be, as I pass the Christmas charity wishing well in the centre. I unfold the tissue paper and once again merrily study the pristine glass, proud of the money I have spent and have saved. How festively-spirited and generous I am!

The clock chimes five o' clock. I freeze in my tracks. Where is the post office? Have I taken the wrong path back home? In a calm panic and packing the present away, I retreat, but the houses all seem different; they are taller, more claustrophobic suddenly. Skidding in a horrifying lurch, I squint in the darkness and the brutal icy pavement winks back. The street lamps have gone out, perhaps due to a power cut, the roads are devoid of cars, and the air smells of rusted machinery and stagnant water. My mind fires cannon after cannon of fears: my family do not know where I am, I cannot be missing on Christmas Day tomorrow, what if something serious happens? Overwhelmingly terrified and confused, I miraculously manage to spot a vaguely familiar house. I shuffle over a stone bridge and hope that someone kind will open the door and help me.

A little girl- with treacle-hair and dark, mischievous chocolate-button-eyes swings the door open. Cheekily grinning, she leaps out of the house and beckons her hands excitedly for me to follow her. Trust instantly waves through my body like sugary syrup, but I am still disorientated.

"Excuse me, do you know the way back to the village?" I ask politely, masking my desperation. She seems to ignore what I say, still smiling and pulling my hand down a street of mismatched buildings, despite the fact that she is only in a thin violet dress and boots in the freezing temperatures. The shops are quaint and divided into places like Greengrocer's and Butcher's- the lettering on the signs hilariously outdated, though of course I am not feeling jovial.

"Where are we going?" I say slowly, worried that her parents are missing her.

She turns back and shakes her head at me, as if I have said something laughable and unintelligent.

"Where are the lampposts?" I turn around in a daze, only familiar with the abnormally clear velvet night sky, "Where are the cash machines and telephone wires and Christmas lights?" She giggles then, yet no sound slips from her mouth.

"Can… can you speak?"

She shakes her head, dragging me faster still with a nimble, fairy-like efficiency.

We pass a wealthy man, wearing a funny tall hat and cane, and the girl snaps her fingers. The very wind seems to holds its breath, motionless. Completely statuette, the girl shakes with laughter and puts a lump of snow under his top hat- clicking again so that he whirls around in the empty road and grumbles as he brushes the abnormally-placed snow away.

Before I can even think about what has happened, she steers me into a Manor House at the end of the scruffy street. "We're breaking in!" I hiss, "someone will catch us!"

She shrugs my suggestion off, unlocking the door with one twist of a finger and skipping inside. Creeping cautiously as if the floorboards will splinter like a sheet of sugared pastry, I absorb the burgundy corridor of framed portraits and antique furniture. Soon it widens out into a spacious kitchen, strung with tinsels of garlic and sprigs of berry baubles.

"Can you show me your name?" I murmur as we slide around the doorway. She pulls a delicate door key from her neck, where it is engraved with *Vivianne*. Without warning, a booming man with an extensive moustache strides into the kitchen, bearing a lit, miniscule match in his hand with a smirk.

"Boys, get to work!" he bellows, moving to thrust the match up the fireplace chimney towards the bare feet.

"Oh, how horrendous!" I blurt out, though he remarkably does not sense us, "Vivianne, this is just like a Victorian history book!"

Her dark eyebrows frown just slightly, blemishing her face like a smudge on a porcelain doll. Purposefully, she clicks her fingers, pausing the man. With one sweep, she lights the man's coattails with the match and it bursts into flames like a prize Christmas pudding.

"What- how?" the man stomps in anger, uselessly patting his back. The chimney sweeps spring forward and quash the flames together, faces painted with soot.

"Ouch… thank you, boys," the master softens, "here, why don't you take some of this food and finish early?"

Delighted, the children stuff their pockets with bread, dashing out of the house in a stampede fuelled by rare liberality. Vivianne beckons me and then we are chasing them too, out of the door and into the clear, chilled night air.

It seems free, charging down the street whilst snowflakes kiss our cheeks, listening to the cheers of the boys, oblivious to the world and the people asleep in their beds as they anticipate the promise of morning. Has the clock in the square stopped ticking? Has time rewound like a backwards train? The freedom narrows in my chest in correlation with the compressed proximity of the makeshift housing. We dart down a tight alleyway, before slipping into a crumbling, granite building. Children line the floor, huddled under scraps of curtains and rags, hair knotted with dirt. Someone hums a carol in the corner, and a simple wreath leans against a thin wall. Incredibly, even here- though where 'here' is I am uncertain- there is a flickering flame of Christmas spirit that cannot be out-sung by the ache of empty stomachs.

"What are we doing here, Vivianne?" I speak to the girl softly, and I cannot tell if she has heard me as she stares timidly around the room, almost uncertain. Instantaneously, her fingers strike like a match, setting the room in a glow. A husband and wife knock on the creaking door. The children burst out of their beds.

"Can it be Christmas morning already, Agatha?" says one scrawny, bleary-eyed boy.

"It is still nightfall," his sister replies. I gaze at the couple curiously, but they both have kindness singing in their eyes.

"Children, our cart has been damaged in the weather, and we will not be able to deliver the neighbourhood's Christmas orders to the Grocer's by morning. If a few of you will help us mend the wheel, we will gladly reward you all with a plentiful feast," the woman pleads hopefully. Scrambling out of bed, the wheel outside is mended by the infants in no time and the cart glides down the road as efficiently and gloriously as a sleigh.

"It's a miracle!" the orphans gasp but, too tired to unbox the gifts left in their doorway, the chattering diminishes and they drift back into a deep sleep.

"Is there any way we can make this place more festive?" I suggest to Vivianne ecstatically. She nods in enthusiastic agreement and, though I suspect her power is limited, a miracle really does take place. Fingers snapping like a flurry of Christmas crackers, Vivianne erupts energy into the dusty room. The wreath becomes adorned with the finest holly and berries, I stream luxurious tinsel across all corners of the room, and a rickety table transforms into a banquet. Rich mince pies, golden roast potatoes, vegetables of every colour, bronzed turkeys and a perfect Christmas pudding adorn the furniture.

"What a surprise this will be when the children wake up," I smile delightedly. Peeking through a blanket of snow clouds, a marzipan sun begins to rise. Hurriedly, Vivianne drags me outside and we are charging back past the mansion, back down the roads, and back over the bridge, far from the shrieks of joy and "Saint Nicholas has been!" in the orphan's shelter. As she goes, she waves her arms over the buildings, leaving presents of woollen scarves and hot food on the doorsteps of poor houses, floating blankets gently over an elderly homeless man on the road.

"Is it time for me to go home?" I ask quietly, though there are a multitude of other burning questions on my mind. Her tiny arms hug me. I have an urge then, to leave everything I own to the people in this poor, humble world, to empty my pockets until every one of the children has a warm home. As I desperately root through my bag for loose change or possessions, tissue paper crinkles against my hand. The girl points to the snow globe, touching it gently. Gradually, the little candlelight beside the figurine glows brighter and brighter, and I know it is time to go back to my Christmas.

Just before everything becomes a white light, I am floating above the city, and I see the house where I met Vivianne; it is the one in the snow globe!

I see her.

The little girl is not in a dress anymore, but an orphan's rags. I see her frail figure kneel upon the desolate doorstep, praying. I see her tiny arms huddle a sheet of fabric around her; it cannot transform into a comfortable bed now. I see her sharing a small piece of bread with the chimney sweeps; they wish each other a "Merry Christmas." I see her offering the last wax of her candle to the homeless man. I see her wave to passers-by, though she does not have the energy to stand and join them. *Look past the globe's glass*. I see through her eyes: the lonely, the sick, the destitute, in every country over the globe, even on the twenty-fifth of December. Amongst the indulgence, I see starvation, amongst the affluence, I see poverty. She watches the world from her doorstep. My mind is lost, frozen, and my tears spin into the swirl of snow cascading over the scene. For the first time, I see outside of the snow globe.

I am back in the present, finally out of my sister's present it would seem. Families laugh and gather around their Christmas trees, exchanging beautiful parcels. The scent of burnt sugar fills my nose: bittersweet. Before I open the front door to my home, I empty my purse into the charity well in the square. Gratefulness and sorrow flurries in my chest. Snow clouds- it will be a special morning for some. I close my eyes and make a wish, as fresh snow falls.

The Siren's Call

by Susan Rocks

I have decided to write down an account of the strange events I experienced in 1972, which have, I believe, had a profound effect on my life. I'll leave you to decide if you believe me, but I swear the events as written here are true.

A naïve twenty year old, I somehow managed to secure a job as a sales rep trying to persuade shopkeepers to stock our particular brand of soft drinks. On my first week unsupervised, I headed for the far west of Dorset for the first time. The threatened storm hit during the afternoon, and I found myself driving down a narrow lane. Rain hammered on the car roof and leaves twisted and twirled, like dead confetti in a whirlwind, making the road slicker, and catching in the flimsy windscreen wipers so they smeared more than cleared. I could barely see the front of my yellow Cortina and I clung to the steering wheel as the water streaming down the narrow lane tried to wrench it from my hands. Branches waved manically overhead, showering twigs onto the car, adding to the cacophony. I crept along slowly, releasing my rigid grip every few minutes to swipe my sleeve across the condensation on the window, which the pathetic heater failed to clear. After what seemed like miles, high hedges replaced the trees and up ahead, the bright white light of a lighthouse pulsed, piercing the gloom. I stopped the car; I shouldn't be this close to the coast. I checked the map but the squiggly lines blurred as my tired eyes strained to make sense of them under the dim interior light. I carried on slowly, searching for a gateway to turn in but the hedges loomed continuously. Heading down a steep hill, the petrol warning light began angrily flashing red, clashing with the lighthouse beams. In the valley, I spotted faint lights, a swinging wooden sign and breathed a sigh of relief. The last thing I needed was to break down in the middle of nowhere. I pulled into the empty pub car park; someone here would point me in the direction of the nearest garage.

By the time I reached the door the rain had plastered my hair to my head and dripped down my neck. My trousers stuck to my legs and water seeped into my cheap shoes. I vowed to be better prepared in future; always carry spare fuel, a decent torch, a mac. I pushed open the heavy oak door and entered a narrow passage, ducking under the low, age-blackened beams. The flagstone floor, worn smooth by thousands of feet, led to another door, light flickering around its edges, and I entered a sparsely furnished room. The bar was on the right-hand side, opposite a large stone fireplace and I was grateful to see a log fire blazing, although the room felt damp, chilled. The walls were that particular shade of ochre, stained by a million cigarettes that no amount of cleaning or repainting could completely erase, the air redolent of tobacco, beer and mildew. Long dead, grumpy fish contained within dusty glass-fronted cases, watched me, and a large oil painting of a shipwreck hung above the fireplace. The only occupant was an elderly man on a stool in the corner. He ignored my entrance, staring into a silver tankard on the bar, fisherman's cap pulled low over a deeply lined face, etched by wind, preserved by sea salt. From somewhere came the sound of laughter, music, faint chatter, as if there was another bar hidden from strangers, in the depths of the building. I hadn't noticed another door and the car park had been empty; no one in their right mind would walk any distance to a pub on a night like this. There must be a village nearby. I could buy petrol and maybe find a room for the night. The man tapped his pipe into an ashtray and began refilling it from a yellow packet he removed from a pocket inside his oilskin jacket.

'Evening,' I said, 'nasty night out there.'

He mumbled something into his tankard and slammed his fist onto the bar, rattling a clutch of smeared glasses awaiting washing. A man emerged through an archway hidden behind a black velvet curtain, wiping a glass with a striped towel. He was tall, well over six feet, and solid, like a rugby player, a thick dark beard, threaded with grey, clasped the lower half of his face, hooded dark eyes were, unwelcoming, forbidding questions.

'Ready for another pint Fred?'

The old man gestured in my direction and I put on my best salesman's smile, practised in the privacy of my bedroom, approaching the bar with outstretched hand. 'Good evening, nasty night out there.' He ignored my hand, placing the glass on the bar,

'Pint? Sir?'

'Oh. Okay. But. I wonder. Could you give me directions to the nearest town? My car's running out of petrol and –'

'S'all closed this time o' night. We got rooms.'

This time of night? It couldn't be much later than five o'clock, although the miserable weather had brought the afternoon to a premature end. I glanced at my watch and saw it was nearly eight o'clock. I tapped it, listened, but it was ticking merrily. Had I really been driving around those lanes for three hours?

'Well, I suppose in that case … do you do food?' No wonder my stomach had been rumbling so ominously; I'd only had a sausage roll and bag of crisps for lunch. The thought of a steaming hot pie or plate of stew in front of the fire felt very appealing, far better than battling through the storm.

'Sandwiches.'

Better than going to bed hungry, I suppose. 'Okay, sounds lovely, thank you.'

'Get yer bags, girl'll show you the room.' He pulled the curtain back a fraction and yelled 'Polly, get in 'ere.'

A young girl appeared, barely a teenager, pale and thin with stringy black hair dangling over her face. I hoped she wasn't preparing the food.

'Show 'im to the back room,' and he vanished behind the curtain.

After fetching my overnight bag from the car and getting another soaking for my trouble, I followed Polly up a narrow flight of stairs and along a corridor to the room at the end. She flicked a switch and, amongst the strange shadows thrown by the shaded wall lights, I saw a large, comfortable looking double bed, a mahogany dresser complete with blue and white china bowl and jug, and a paisley print wing-backed chair beside the casement window. Polly produced a box of matches and lit the fire in the small fireplace, prodding it with an iron poker as the flames caught the kindling.

'Bath's two doors down,' she told her feet, and backed out of the room. I shivered and went to the window. The wind howled around the corner of the building, rattling the panes, finding minute gaps to creep through, bringing the sharp tang of ozone into the room. During a brief lull in the wind, I heard the sea crashing against the rocks below. The lighthouse still flashed its warning and I noticed the occasional flash and flare of car headlights in the lane. Odd, I hadn't seen another vehicle for miles, but there were several passing the inn as if they were oblivious to it. I felt a sudden sense of unreality and if I closed my eyes, I could picture Dick Turpin galloping up on his horse. I must be more tired than I thought. I pulled the heavy damask curtains closed but they did little to stop the draught. I washed quickly and pulled on a dry sweater and jeans, leaving my wet shoes propped on the hearth, hoping they would be dry by morning. The fire was doing little to dispel the chill, damp air so I prodded it and put a couple of logs on top of the smouldering kindling, before returning to the bar.

Fred was still staring into his tankard, pipe smoke loitering around his head.

'Is there a pay phone here?' I asked. I'd promised to phone my Mum when I could as she worried about me. Fred removed his pipe long enough to take a long swallow of beer, replaced it firmly and puffed out more smoke. Obviously not interested in conversation. The barman appeared through the curtain, carrying a pint of beer and plate of ham sandwiches.

'There you go,' he placed them in front of me and turned to leave.

'Excuse me, I thought I heard music, is there another bar?'

'Nope.' And he was gone.

'Why don't you join me?' I turned and suddenly the room felt warm, welcoming. She sat at a table next to the fire, the most beautiful woman I had ever seen. How had I not noticed her when I came in?

I felt my face heat. 'Oh. That's very k-kind of you. Th-thanks.' Beer and sandwiches forgotten I moved towards her, helpless under her gaze, as if caught in a net being hauled ashore. There was a bottle of champagne in an ice bucket on the table. She filled two glasses and passed me one.

'To fellow travellers,' she smiled, raising her glass to me. I willed my hand to move as I studied her. Her blonde hair cascaded down her back, mingling with her shimmering pale gold dress; the embodiment of the glass of champagne. Her eyes were the colour of the sea on the sunniest of days and the reflections of the flickering flames flashed in them as she smiled at me. A gossamer fine scarf, the exact shade of blue as her eyes, caressed her throat. I no longer heard the faint voices from the hidden room. I no longer smelt Fred's pipe smoke. Her perfume, light, floral that brought to mind a summer's day, with faint undertones of the sea, surrounded me.

We talked, I know that. I don't remember what we talked about, if I ate my supper, or how much we drank. We laughed, I don't remember about what. We clicked, there's no other word for it. I'm loathe to say it was love at first sight but I don't know how else to describe the feelings I experienced that night. Finally, she stood, rising in a singular fluid movement and I noticed her dress hugged her figure in all the right places, and skimmed the floor, hiding her feet.

‘Come,’ she said, extending her hand. Her skin was smooth, cool and I stood hurriedly, my chair scraping the flagstones, an unholy screech, that failed to break the spell. I followed her up the stairs to my room in a daze.

The following morning I woke alone. All that remained was the faintest hint of her perfume on the pillow. Pale dawn light crept around the edges of the curtain as I stretched and yawned, feeling as if I had slept for days. I dressed hurriedly, hoping she was already downstairs organising breakfast as I was famished. Outside, the sky was clear, the trees still above the mist which hovered over the ground. I could now see that the inn nestled in a dip between two headlands, watched over by the lighthouse. High above a murmuration of starlings swept black patterns across the sky, as if from an artist’s brush. I swiftly packed my case and rushed down to the bar. Fred was still in his corner, drinking coffee, newspaper propped against the beer pumps.

‘Good morning,’ I exclaimed, far too loud, ‘lovely day!’

Fred thumped the bar and the landlord appeared through the curtain.

‘Good morning. Has my … companion arranged breakfast?’ Embarrassed, I realised I didn’t know her name.

‘Don’t do breakfast. Bill sir?’

'Oh. Maybe a cup of coffee please? If it's not too much trouble?'

He slipped his hand behind the curtain like a magician, and pulled out a cup and saucer, placing it on the bar, then took a pad from his pocket and laboriously wrote my bill.

'Has my lady friend left already?' I hoped she had left me a note, her phone number, something.

'And what lady would that be sir?'

'The lady I was with last night. Here.' I pointed to the table where we had spent the evening.

'No sir. You ate your food and retired alone.'

'No. She was sitting there and asked me to join her. Wasn't she Fred? You s-saw her didn't you?' Fred mumbled into his coffee cup. 'M-maybe's she's in the other bar?'

'No sir. No other bar, no other customers.'

His words scrambled in my brain. Nothing made sense.

'B-but –'

'Your bill sir,' and he pushed it across the bar.

I froze under his hostile stare. I remember I took some money from my wallet and he must have given me a receipt because I still have it. I went out to my car wondering if it had been a dream. Could it? It had seemed so real. Was I that tired last night? Everything seemed blurred, as if seen through murky glasses. Without even consulting my map, I turned onto the lane and, within five minutes, pulled into a garage forecourt on the edge of the town I had been unable to find the previous night.

After fuelling the car, I walked across the road to a café and ordered a full English and pot of tea. The waitress, a chatty, motherly type, asked what I was doing in the area. I told her I'd spent the night at the inn back along the road and she laughed.

'The Mermaid? Don't think so love. It's been derelict for years, ever since the tragedy.'

'I didn't notice the name,' I said. 'It was old, in the valley below the lighthouse. No more than five minutes away.'

'No. You must mean the Kings Head,' and she named a village I remembered from the previous day.

'No. It was The Mermaid …' She stared at me as if I'd grown two heads and turned to go. 'Wait. Sorry, you're right. I must be mistaken. I'm new to this area. What was the tragedy you mentioned?'

She told me about a terrible storm one night, some forty years ago. The inn was busy as usual and during the evening, a woman had rushed in, begging for help as her husband's ship had run aground on the rocks. Naturally, everyone followed her down to the shore, but, as they reached the ship a colossal wave reared up and swept the landlord, his young daughter, and one of the local fishermen away. When the others finally got aboard the stricken ship they found the crew all dead, and there was no sign of the woman. The landlord's family moved away and no one wanted to take on the inn, so they boarded it up. Some of the old fishermen recalled similar things happening in the past, but my friendly waitress was sceptical.

'I mean, it's an old building love. And folks like telling tales don't they? Parents make up all sorts of stories to scare their kiddies away from dangerous places, like derelict buildings. Or to frighten the little ones at Halloween!'

'What was the woman like? Do you know?'

'Gracious lovey, how should I know! Long before my time. Though they do say a woman's seen sitting by the shore during storms, but I don't believe it. More tea?'

I left in a daze, driving back to the inn which was indeed, boarded up. Ivy was gradually overtaking the brickwork, and one of the chimneys had smashed in pieces across the weed-strewn car park. I don't know how long I sat there, appointments forgotten, simply staring at the inn. The weather was closing in again, turning the world sepia as the mist thickened, rolling in from the sea. Finally I concluded I must have slept in the car, the weird dream triggered by the strange surroundings and the vicious storm. Remembering the petrol receipt, I added it to the growing pile in the coin tray by the gear lever and noticed the one on top; The Mermaid Inn. A glimpse of blue caught my eye then, peeping from under the passenger seat. I leant down and withdrew a scarf, light as a butterfly's wing, the colour of the sea on the sunniest of days.

I never did make my appointments that day, and was sacked not long afterwards. My life in the thirty years since that night hasn't exactly been as I had envisioned. First, and devastatingly, my beloved Mum died unexpectedly the following year. I have been unable to sustain any serious relationship; no woman has ever managed to match my mysterious lover. I've drifted from job to job, still a salesman driving up and down the country. I often come back here especially when a bad storm's forecast. There's a bench in front of the lighthouse, with a plaque commemorating all the souls lost at sea, and I make the long climb up from the new car park to sit and wait. I'm drawn here, as I was drawn to her so long ago. Or maybe I'm hoping one day she will return. At low tide, when the normally concealed rocks can be seen in all their vicious glory, I often think I see her, sitting, watching for ships. But it's my imagination.

It's getting cold now, the wind's growing stronger. Starlings are swooping and weaving overhead and ominously dark clouds are approaching across the sea. Soon the lighthouse will begin flashing its warning. Hang on, there is someone on the rocks. It's not my imagination. I'm going to pause writing to take a closer look as I think it's a blonde woman. Can it be her? After all this time? She's waving, beckoning me to join her. I'll leave this journal here while I go to the edge and take a closer look…

New Neighbours

by Jeff Jones

Despondency washed over Jenny as their car pulled into Maddison Lane and it wasn't just because of the torrential rain and thunderstorm which seemed to have stalked them all the way from the airport. Most people felt a bit down after coming home from a holiday, it was only natural, but this was different somehow. She knew that she had no right to feel depressed. They'd enjoyed a relaxing two weeks sunning themselves whilst most people had spent their gloomy, December days fighting their way through the crowds shopping for Christmas presents. Even the flight home, which was normally a subdued and melancholy affair, had been fun with the cabin crew doing their best to make it feel festive with Christmas songs piped over the speakers and crackers supplied with their meals. Add to that the fact that both she and Mark had fantastic jobs to come home to and that they'd just moved into a lovely new house a few weeks before they'd gone away meant she really was at a loss to explain her mood. As they neared their driveway, however, Jenny suddenly realised what it was that was dragging her down; it was the foreboding house that sat directly opposite theirs.

There was nothing wrong with the house, in fact they'd viewed it themselves before finally settling on the one they now lived in, but it just hadn't felt right. She'd loved the location, the layout, and the great sprawling landscaped gardens, but something had felt off. She hadn't been able to explain it and Mark had been disappointed, but in the end he'd acquiesced to her wish to look elsewhere, anything for a quieter life. The reason for her unease she'd later found out, was probably due to the fact that about a hundred years earlier a previous owner had murdered her husband and two children before hanging herself from the lovely oak tree which stood on the front lawn.

When Jenny had found out, she had tersely informed the estate agent that she was no longer interested in the property though it had broken her heart to do so, and promptly dispensed with his services. Luckily, the house opposite had come onto the market shortly after and whilst it wasn't quite as quaint or old, it was still very nice. They'd pitched an insultingly low offer for the house but instead of rejecting it out of hand the owners had accepted it and within just six weeks they had completed and moved in. It was as if the previous owners couldn't wait to leave.

"New neighbours I see," said Mark breaking her reverie.

She was so lost in her own thoughts Jenny hadn't noticed that they were finally home.

"Sorry, what?"

"I said I see we've finally got new neighbours." Mark jabbed his thumb back towards the house opposite.

Jenny swivelled in her seat and saw that he was right. Faint lights glowed within the house, though there was no sign of a car on the driveway.

"That's good. Must have just moved in because the 'Sold' board's still up. Not a good start though."

"What do you mean?" asked Mark.

"Well there must have been a power cut because that looks like candlelight to me, not electric lights."

"Can't be unless it's localised to just their house – the street lamps are still on. They're probably just getting in the mood for Christmas and going all atmospheric."

"Maybe. I just hope our power's on, I could murder a coffee."

"Sounds good. Anyway, at least now you can stop worrying."

"I wasn't worrying," replied Jenny indignantly. "I just didn't like the idea of the house unoccupied what with its sordid history and everything. Besides, it's bad for an area if a house remains unoccupied for very long."

"If you say so. Now come on, let's get this lot inside, grab a coffee and get to bed – I'm knackered. Feel like I need a holiday to get over the holiday."

An hour later, Jenny stood at the large bay window in their bedroom and stared over at the house opposite. The house was completely dark now the occupants having presumably gone to bed. Whether it was the house's history or the storm which showed no sign of abating, she wasn't sure, but the place really gave her the creeps. Whether she'd have felt the same way had she not known about its history she couldn't tell.

A huge flash of lightning briefly illuminated everything in front of her, making Jenny jump and for a split second she thought she saw people staring back at her from an upstairs window. The huge crash of thunder that followed made her scream and after hastily yanking the curtains together, she ran across the room and leapt into bed, much to Mark's amusement.

"Since when did you get scared of a little storm?"

"Ever since we moved opposite the house of horrors, that's when."

"Bit extreme isn't it? I thought you loved the place."

"That was before I found out what happened in there. Besides, I'm sure they were just staring over at me from an upstairs window."

"Who?"

"The new neighbours. Who did you think I meant?"

"Dunno. The way you're acting it could have meant anybody."

"Well I meant them. It looked like a woman and two small children but it happened so fast I couldn't tell for certain."

"Well they can't see us now so turn the light off and let's get some sleep."

Jenny reached over and turned the lamp off before snuggling down under the reassuringly cosy duvet.

"Kind of weird don't you think, the way they were just staring over here?"

"What, more than you standing at the window staring over at them you mean? They're probably wondering what kind of crazy lady they've moved opposite to."

He had a point.

"Whatever. Anyway, I'll go and introduce myself tomorrow and see if there's anything they need and whilst I'm doing that you can put our Christmas decorations up," and with that Jenny rolled over and soon drifted off, though it was to be anything but a restful night's sleep. Images of people staring at her from dark recesses and thunderstorms that never ended blighted her night and it was a tired and irritable Jenny who woke a few hours later.

After unpacking their suitcases, and making sure that Mark was definitely going to put the decorations up and not just lie around on the sofa, Jenny finally summoned the courage to walk over and introduce herself to their new neighbours. As she crunched her way up the shingle driveway and looked about her at the magnificent gardens, she was unable to subdue the pangs of regret that gnawed away at her stomach. Nor was she able to shake the feeling that she was being watched. The temptation to glance up at the upstairs windows was almost overpowering. Instead she glanced left at the towering oak tree which dominated that part of the lawn. A cry of alarm escaped her mouth when out of the corner of her eye she would have sworn she saw somebody hanging from one of its lower branches. Eyes wide with terror and with a hand clamped over her mouth, Jenny spun fully to face the tree but this time there was nothing there.

Shaking, and bitterly regretting her decision to come over, she turned back to face the house. She couldn't leave now because if she had been seen, it would make for a very awkward first encounter at some future point. Plus Mark would laugh her out of town. She climbed up onto the porch and admired the tastefully decorated miniature fir trees stood either side of the front door like sentinels – a nice touch she thought. These weren't cheap decorations from a pound store, but quality ones from one of the more upmarket shops. The new owners obviously had taste. The holly wreath that adorned the front door was beautiful but it was the door itself which caught Jenny's attention. She was positive that when they'd viewed the property several months before, the house had a new plastic door, incongruous to the rest of the building for sure, but ultimately more practical. The door in front of her now, however, was a weather-beaten wooden one with a heavy cast iron knocker in the shape of a lion's head. It seemed the new owners were trying to maintain the house's period look, which was probably a good thing.

Jenny took a deep calming breath and then banged the knocker several times. It gave a resounding clang that would surely have woken the dead let alone anyone in the house. That, she realised, was an unsettling thought given the house's history. Try as she might she couldn't shake the feeling of uneasiness and took an instinctive pace back giving herself room to manoeuvre if she didn't like whatever answered the door. As she waited, she shifted her weight from one foot to the other. Her hands felt clammy and she tried to wipe them dry on her jeans, but to no avail. There was no immediate answer yet she was sure someone was in. She could feel it. When she'd walked up the driveway she had been certain she'd seen a flicker of movement from within and the twitching of a curtain upstairs.

She knocked again and after waiting what she considered an appropriate length of time it was with some relief that she turned to walk home. She let out a gasp of surprise when she nearly bumped into a woman stood right behind her.

"I'm sorry I didn't mean to startle you. I was in the back garden and thought I heard somebody knock, so came round to investigate," said the woman. She was plainly dressed apart from a silk scarf which adorned her neck, yet elegant and spoke with a well-to-do accent.

"That's all right, you just made me jump. My name's Jenny, I live opposite you," said Jenny pointing needlessly towards her house. "I thought I'd come over and introduce myself as we're going to be neighbours." She offered her hand to shake.

"Nice to meet you, Jenny. My name's Elizabeth. I'd shake your hand but..." she held up her muddy gloves apologetically.

It was no big deal, but Jenny couldn't help wondering why the woman didn't simply remove a glove to shake her hand. What was she hiding? Perhaps she just didn't welcome human contact. It would certainly explain why she'd bought one of two isolated houses.

"I'm so glad you've moved in," said Jenny. "It was depressing looking at an empty house all day. It's lovely around here but it can be a bit lonely. And you've moved in just in time for Christmas, too. How lovely."

"Yes, I love it too. I can't see us ever leaving."

"Do you need anything? We've not been here long ourselves and haven't completely unpacked yet, but I'm sure if you need something I should be able to lay my hands on it."

"That's very kind of you, Jenny, but we're fine."

An awkward silence suddenly filled the air. Clearly Elizabeth wasn't going to invite her in for an ice-breaking coffee so Jenny decided to beat a dignified retreat. She'd already made her mind up that she didn't particularly like this woman anyway.

"Okay, good. If you change your mind you know where to find me." Jenny smiled and stepped past Elizabeth towards her own house, her gaze briefly falling on the oak tree, which she was relieved to see had nothing hanging from it. After a couple of paces she stopped and turned. "Incidentally, Elizabeth, I hope you don't mind me asking, but are you aware of the history of your house?" A strange look flickered across Elizabeth's face, but it New neighbours quickly disappeared. "The only reason I ask is that we were going to buy this house until we found out what happened. The estate agent didn't tell us but we found out anyway. Apparently a woman stabbed her husband to death when she found out he'd been having an affair. Then she killed her children before hanging herself. All on Christmas Day would you believe?" *Bet you wish you'd invited me in for a coffee now.* If she'd been hoping for some sort of shocked reaction from Elizabeth, she was out of luck. *Probably already knew,* reasoned Jenny, suddenly feeling spiteful for mentioning it in the first place.

"Yes, I'd heard something along those lines, but I don't talk about it as I don't wish to frighten the children."

Jenny's feeling of guilt increased ten-fold. She'd forgotten she'd seen two small children standing next to the woman in the window the previous night. "Yes, of course, I understand and they won't hear about it from me. Anyway, when you're unpacked and settled after Christmas perhaps you'd all like to come over for a drink and meet my husband Mark?"

"Perhaps."

Don't kill yourself; I'm not that bothered, thought Jenny irritated by the woman's lack of enthusiasm at her attempt to offer friendship. It was an offer she wouldn't repeat.

"Okay, good." It was getting really awkward now. "Well, I'll leave you to carry on. It was nice meeting you and I wish you all a merry Christmas."

"Thank you. You too."

Jenny turned and made her way off the porch and back down the shingle driveway walking as fast as common decency allowed, keen to put as much distance between herself and the woman as she could. Halfway down she couldn't resist turning to take another look and was disturbed to find the woman still standing on the porch watching her go. She was flanked on either side by her two small children. Feeling awkward Jenny raised her hand and waved. They didn't wave back. Jenny turned and hurried home vowing that she wouldn't return without company.

Over the next few days Jenny tried to keep a low profile still feeling awkward about their earlier encounter. Elizabeth had never taken up her invitation or even just popped over for a cup of tea and Jenny began to wonder whether she had really offended her. Mark had told her to stop worrying saying that perhaps they were the type of people who liked to keep themselves to themselves and Jenny had reluctantly accepted his explanation.

Every now and again though Jenny would catch a glimpse of Elizabeth and a man she took to be her husband. Once or twice she also thought she saw the children, a young boy and girl. None of them seemed to ever leave the grounds of the house and Jenny still hadn't clapped eyes on a car. Nor had they received any visitors, though there was a whole host of explanations for that.

One day Jenny had been raking leaves in the front garden when the sound of children giggling had caught her attention. Thinking this might be a way to reignite communication between the two families, Jenny had crossed the road to talk to them, but by the time she reached the bottom of their driveway, both had disappeared though she felt she was being watched.

Perhaps Mark is right and they just like their privacy. If that's how they want it, so be it I'll leave them alone. They know where I am if they change their minds.

But to Mark's annoyance she couldn't leave it alone. Their neighbours' unwillingness to engage with them irritated Jenny and watching their house for signs of activity was fast becoming an obsession.

"Will you come away from the window and give it a rest for crying out loud?" said Mark irritably. "It's nearly Christmas; why don't you come to bed and give me an early Christmas present?" He patted the empty bed beside him for good effect but it was a wasted gesture as she never turned round and instead kept her gaze fixed upon the house opposite.

"In a minute," Jenny snapped back.

"Don't you see you're becoming obsessed?"

"I'm not becoming obsessed; don't be ridiculous."

"This from the woman stood at the bedroom window watching the neighbours through binoculars. And why? Because they won't pop over for a drink or invite us over. So what? Now come to bed."

"In a minute I said."

"Have you ever thought they just might not like us?"

"I've only ever spoken to her and they've never met you, so no I haven't. Besides, what's not to like?" replied Jenny finally turning to face her husband, a small grin tugging at the corners of her mouth.

Just then a scream pierced the night air followed by frightened shouting. Jenny thought she could hear a child scream. She spun round again and put the binoculars to her eyes.

"Did you hear that?" she asked, scanning from window to window but unable to make anything out.

"Yes, I did," and even as he replied the sound of more shouting drifted in through their partially open window.

"Should we call the police?"

"Why? They're just having an argument. It happens."

"Some argument if we can hear it over here. And what about the scream? That child sounded petrified."

"What about it?"

"He might be hurting her, or worse still the kids."

"You don't know that. I'm telling you it's probably just a normal argument, now come away from the window and leave it be. If one of them spots you it'll only make things worse."

"But..."

"Leave it... please."

Reluctantly Jenny put the binoculars down and climbed into bed, immediately turning her back on him. His slim chance of an early amorous Christmas present had all but evaporated thanks to the neighbours, and he silently cursed them.

"If she's got a black eye or something the next time I see her, I'm holding you responsible, Mark. Those poor kids – it's Christmas Eve tomorrow and they should be excited about Christmas but instead they have to put up with their parents fighting." She lay awake for some time listening for more tell-tale signs of trouble but none came yet it was still some time before she finally nodded off.

A few hours later, Jenny was woken by the sound of a large vehicle pulling up in the road outside.

An ambulance! I knew I should have called the police.

Wrapping her dressing gown around her she padded over to the window and pulled the curtain back, the sudden burst of sunlight stirring Mark from his slumber.

Just turning into the driveway opposite was not an ambulance as she'd suspected, but a large truck with the words *Danny's Removals,* emblazoned on the side, closely followed by two cars.

"What's going on?" asked Mark blearily.

"They're moving."

"Who is?"

"The lot opposite."

"What?" said Mark incredulously, sitting up in bed. "They've only just moved in."

"Perhaps that's what they were fighting about last night. She told me she couldn't ever see them leaving that place. Maybe her husband's forcing them all to move and things came to a head last night. I'm going out to speak to Elizabeth."

Before Mark could stop her, she threw on some clothes, shot out of the bedroom, down the stairs and out into the street, where she stood glancing anxiously around for Elizabeth. She then made her way up the driveway towards where the vehicles had parked and a where bustle of activity was already unfolding.

"I'm really sorry, we didn't mean to wake you, but we've got so much to do we had to get an early start," said a girl's voice behind Jenny.

Jenny spun round and saw an attractive blonde girl in her early thirties smiling at her.

"My name's Carla and the bloke over there in the blue shirt is my husband Steve," said the girl extending her hand.

Jenny shook the proffered hand. "Hi, I'm Jenny. I'm sorry, you're moving in where?"

Carla nodded at the house to their right wondering where else Jenny thought she could be moving in to considering there were only two houses nearby and the removal men were already unloading the truck. The woman looked exhausted and Carla put the stupidity of her question down to tiredness. "Here. Steve and I have had some relationship problems and needed to make a fresh start." *Because my cheating husband couldn't keep his hands off that bitch next door,* she thought bitterly to herself.

"Oh! You're moving in with Elizabeth and her family?" said Jenny suddenly feeling foolish and a little embarrassed at the other woman's candour about her marriage problems with a complete stranger.

"In a matter of speaking I suppose, yes, though I hope they're not around much," replied Carla giggling.

"Well this house is big enough for all of you I think. Do you have kids?" asked Jenny glancing around.

"No, we don't."

"Well at least you'll have Elizabeth's around you; they should keep you on your toes." She was surprised that Elizabeth and her family weren't already outside greeting what was presumably their family. Maybe they were supervising the removal men indoors.

"I certainly hope not," said Carla laughing nervously.

"Oh, I'm sorry, I must have misunderstood. I assumed you liked kids."

"I do. I just prefer flesh and blood rather than unhappy ghosts. I'm weird that way."

"I'm sorry I don't understand."

"I know you probably think we're mad to move in on the anniversary of Looney Liz's killing spree, but it's just the way it worked out being part of a chain. Christmas Eve isn't ideal to be moving in but it's kind of romantic I suppose."

Jenny stared blankly back at Carla.

"You do know what happened in this house, right?" asked Carla.

"The murders, yes," replied Jenny.

"That's right. One of the previous owners, an Elizabeth Hallington, found out her husband was cheating on her and stabbed him and her two children to death before hanging herself from that tree over there. I think it's a hundred and two years ago today funny enough." *Perhaps I'll do the same if Steve doesn't keep it in his pants from now on.* "Anyway, it was nice meeting you. I'd better go or Steve will moan that's he's doing all the work."

Jenny smiled weakly and watched as the removal men began to carry some furniture and boxes through the front door, except that it was no longer the old-fashioned wooden front door of a few days ago, but the modern one she remembered from their house viewing.

Sensing she was once again being watched, Jenny glanced towards the upstairs windows and wasn't surprised to see Elizabeth, what had to be her husband and two small children staring down at her. What she wasn't expecting was to see their clothes soaked in fresh looking blood. Elizabeth's neck also lolled at an odd angle on her shoulders and without the silk scarf, Jenny could see a livid purple line around her throat.

Her eyes wide with shock, Jenny looked round for someone to share the horror with, but when she glanced back up they had disappeared. With one last look at the scene before her, Jenny hurried back down the driveway, across the street and into her house wondering what time the estate agent opened.

The Cogs of Time

by Bruno Kalmar

(Children's Highly Commended)

The man walks slowly, with the utmost care, rhythmically putting one foot in front of the other. Leather boots encase his feet, which is bruised from the neverending walking and neglect. Still, he is determined; *willing* to walk, to brave the dangerous wending pathways. He cannot stop. He isn't a spectacle, though people try to make him out as one. After all, svelte is just another word for malnourished and pale another word for sickly. The deep, blue eyes, however, are not an exaggeration. They draw you in like the sea in tranquillity, then, tumult. The waves break out, hammering you down with massive force. Drowning you slowly, patiently waiting as you run out of breath, becoming of less and less importance. The eyes are his personality. His personality are his eyes. *You must never fear.*

Meandering along the constant pathways, he thinks about what would happen if he were to stop. Hunted, caught and taken back to nuclear shelter BL 137, where he would carry on celebrating Christmas with people who are blinded by dogma and stupidity. Best case scenario is that he is killed by the government. Supercilious idiots. *Never Fear.* He would refuse to celebrate Christmas without the knowledge of where her body is. Marlynn. A longtime friend, who vanishes. A smart and witty person. Killed in the nuclear explosion or killed by the government. It doesn't matter after all. Knowledge was why she was left to be killed. Knowledge is power. *You must never fear.*

Howling winds ruffle his hair, moving it slightly. Here he is, looking for a body during christmas, when he could be safe inside a nuclear shelter, yet, he persists. *Never Fear.* Bomb begin to rain, shrapnel and detritus flying about as hues of red and orange painted the dark canvas of the sky. The bombing makes no difference to the barren landscape. He thinks to himself humming softly, as bombs snake behind him. *Never Fear.* The colours dance a deadly bolero, competing amongst themselves for the nicest hue. *Never Fear.* He takes in the destruction, the deadly bombs closing in. He must not stop. *Never Fear.* Yet, he does. He stops. Sits down. A strong force takes him by surprise. *A Bomb.* Bleeding, he begins to black out, yet he cannot. He must be alive. He must keep on fighting, battling against the Machiavellian forces of nature. *A figure of white and shades materialises and stands there. Yet you do not realise.* He perks up, hearing the voice and he is taken by surprise.

"Marlynn!" He yells in his surprisingly low voice, looking up at the figure of white and shades, filling himself with hope although he is bleeding. *Yes, 'tis me,* replies the figure of white and shades, voice supposedly emanating from the man's head. "Where are you? Why are you?

What are you?" asks the man quizzically, his black hair shining in the sinister dance of hues. *I am the ghost of fates, the voice inside your head. You must cease making the effort. You must stop. You must stop now.* The figure of white and shades knows that the man still has a desire to live beside her. *You can become a ghost, with great pain. Eternally, you can see your loved ones die. Alcaeus. Don't stay. Leave.* The man looks up. No-one has called him by his name in a long time.

Alcaeus. The bombs rain harder. *This could be your last Christmas. Learn. Know when to give up. You will live, and be badly wounded. Your dignity and your strength.* The figure of white and shadows disappears. Slowly, the bombs rain harder, hitting Alcaeus. He falls, slowly through the void between life and death. The bombs are of small significance. Blackness. *Yet, he becomes a ghost.* His body shimmers, vanishes, a figure of white and shades appears above it. Time speeds up, physically whirring by. The two figures of white and shades look at each other, the eyes of Alcaeus no longer blue, but white. The two ghosts lock into a seemingly eternal gaze as Alcaeus is transported through time, which whirrs by in a non-existent motion. Dropping from overhead, bombs still whiz about, banging like crackers. The planet erodes, slowly grinded by the cogs of time, till there is nothing. *Yes, we ghosts can see the future and are eternal. We must withstand the emptiness of time, squatting eternally. You are unlucky. You could have died and been forgotten about, but here you are. Take heed of advice from ghosts and fate. You could have celebrated Christmas happily and with gay abandon, but, you do not.* And with that, both ghosts disappear, tracking back in time, leaving you, the dear reader, here, watching as time play out.

The Sea Fret

by Tricia Lyon

All week we had gone down early to the beach, before the crowds arrived. We had a picnic breakfast and played until it got busy, then left to do something more interesting for grownups during the day. We always went back in the evening for a last walk or swim so, despite their attempts to look pathetic, no child- or dog- had been short changed on the beach front this holiday. But we promised them that we would spend all of the last day there.

'Are you ready? What's keeping you?' Mark stood in the doorway holding his snorkelling gear. The children had buckets and spades, also toys hidden in bulging pockets. I was carrying the picnic food, several changes of clothes, swimsuits, towels and all the other paraphernalia needed for a full day on the beach; wet wipes and plastic bags included. I scowled but Mark just grinned, and took most of the stuff from me.

Our favourite beach was a long walk from the carpark but that kept the crowds away. I had visited it often in my childhood and was delighted that my family was enchanted by it too. It was still quiet as we straggled across to the far side, the dog frolicking around us, the children collecting shells. The tide was on its way out, the sand still cold and firm; a few hours yet to low tide. We bagged our favourite spot, tucked in a curve of the low cliffs, on a ridge of sand that this week remained just above the high-water level. A little stream ran past, all that was left of what had once been a creek leading up to the village. When the tide was high the children could boogie board along it on the fast, incoming swell. We paddled, dammed the stream and made sand sculptures, a dolphin, a car, and a turtle. By late morning the beach was busy and the children had found friends to play with.

I got out my drawing kit and tried to sketch the children as they played. Josh was now eight and as I drew I began to see how he might look as an adult. Jamie still had a rounded baby-ness about him despite his desperation to be grown up and do everything his brother did. Mark stood up, flippers in hand,

'I'm going snorkelling, I should be able to go around the headland at low tide.'

'Bring back a crab for supper then.'

It was a standing joke, he had never worked out how to carry one and swim at the same time. And maybe he couldn't face killing it either. Soon I heard sounds of a squabble developing, Jamie was being picked on and Josh couldn't allow that, only he got to hassle his little brother,

'Lunchtime, food, come and get it.'

That gave them an excuse to escape their new friends with no loss of honour. They helped spread out the picnic, getting sand in most of the food. Mark was going to love that. After we had eaten, cleaned up, and the boys had peed in a quiet corner, I looked at my sketches. Josh definitely had a look of my brother Dan about him now, the turn of his head, the shy smile when he glanced up at me.

Daniel had been missing for years, he'd gone to Australia to work and had just vanished. My father thought he had run away from his debts, which Dad had refused to pay. As the years passed I think my parents worried that they should have paid them, that maybe Dan had been in deeper trouble than we'd known. My father refused to discuss the matter, my mother feared he had been killed. But I hoped he was still out there somewhere. I realised that this week he had been missing for seven years, so now he would be declared dead. I turned away from the boys to hide the tears that suddenly streamed down my face. I longed to see Dan again if only for once; just to know he was happy would be enough.

I shivered as I tried to banish my gloomy thoughts which were too miserable for the last day of our holiday. But the weather had changed, becoming cool as a thin layer of cloud covered the sun and a mist spread up the beach. People began to pack up and leave, disappointed at the loss of sunshine. I smiled inwardly, feeling slightly superior; this was just a sea fret, brought on by the change of tide. In half an hour, it would be sunny again. We just needed to wear our jumpers for a while.

As the mist got thicker and rolled closer to us I became uneasy. I wished Mark would come back, I didn't like him to be floating about the headland in this fog. I had never seen a fret this dense before, it had become seriously cold too. As Josh and I stuffed various bits of kit into our bags, Jamie let out a cry; the sea of icy air had engulfed him, hiding him from view. I ducked down into it and searched for him by feel, unable to see anything. I caught hold of him and felt he was being tugged away from me. I picked him up and held him high above me out of the swirling cold as I looked about for Josh, fearful he too would be swept away.

'Josh, get up onto the rocks, quick!'

Josh was already scrambling up the shallow cliff. I thrust Jamie up above my head and he grabbed him then together they climbed higher as I abandoned our bags and followed them. We huddled together on a grassy ledge, the dog tucked in the middle, shivering despite his dense, curly grey fur. I tried to be cheerful, burbling nonsense to the boys,

'What an adventure, I wonder if we'll see any smugglers?'

But Jamie was starting to whimper and even Josh was almost in tears. I grew more anxious. If this was just a sea fret, why was my heart pounding so loudly? I rationalised that it was because every other noise had been blotted out. Then the silence was broken by the faint sound of oars dipping and pulling and the slap of water against the sides of a dinghy. An old dinghy with shabby paint, coming out of the mist. There were four men rowing and one at the tiller, moving steadily on the tide of cold, heading up the creek at the side of the beach. We watched as they drew past us, mesmerised by the rhythm of their oars. The rowers kept their heads down but tillerman glanced up and smiled gently. Then the boat slipped into the mist and was gone.

'Cronk, cronk.' The call of a raven broke the spell; I looked up and saw him perched just a little way above us, his dark, intelligent eyes watching us. He called again as he rose into the air and flew after the dinghy. As the cloud began to thin the sun showed through as a pale disc. I turned to look at the creek but it, and the dinghy, had vanished along with the fret. Down the beach the tide had just turned and through the remaining mist I could just see Mark's outline, flippers in hand, striding towards us, jaunty in the way he only is when he's been playing in the sea. Jamie yelled,

'Daddy, we saw a boat with pirates!'

'Really, real pirates?'

'Um, maybe,' Josh muttered as he scrambled down the rocks, 'it was cool.'

He wasn't going to admit how scared we all had been. The sun re-appeared fully and warmed us as I passed Jamie down to Mark, feeling foolish at my earlier distress, yet my feeling of unease remained. Josh spread out a blanket and opened the picnic bag, then got out the flask of hot chocolate and poured out generous cups for us all. As he looked up to see if I approved he smiled and I gasped. He looked just like the tillerman.

The Haunting of the General

by Emily Dibbs

When Adelia awoke screaming for the third time, her mother's anger burst with the violence of the previous evening's fireworks.

"Stop this!" she hissed, her nose almost touching her daughter's. "You will wake your father's guests. If you insist on having these bad dreams every time you close your eyes, you would do better not to sleep at all!"

Adelia swallowed the last remnants of her shriek. Despite what her mother said, she didn't think that nightmares were causing her fear. The terror only rose in her when she struggled to wake up, as if there was something horrifying about re-entering the waking world. Her mother huffed and turned over on the bed beside her. Part of her irritation, Adelia knew, was the humiliation at being ousted to her daughter's bedroom. Their grand house was large, but not quite large enough to accommodate the mob of important gentleman her father had invited to stay for the New Year's celebrations, hoping to secure investment in his ailing insurance business. Her mother was forced into giving up her room and left with the option of sharing either with her husband or her only daughter. No choice at all, really.

Once her mother's breaths steadied into the rhythm of sleep, Adelia slipped out from under the covers and placed her feet on the floor beside the bed. She did not wish to return to that place between waking and sleeping where an indistinct terror had lurked for the last couple of nights. She wrapped a shawl around her shoulders and stepped out onto the landing. The electric chandelier at the end of the corridor blazed brightly, its light casting a pretty glow on the festive foliage tucked around the frames of the portraits lining the walls. Adelia set off towards the drawing room, navigating each staircase with care for fear of squeaks that might send a maid running.

The only light in the drawing room came from the moon outside the window. The embers in the fireplace had long since burned out, and her breath puffed in white plumes. Adelia sat at the piano forte. Her shoulders prickled with something sharper than the cold, and she glanced nervously around the room. Satisfied it was empty, she turned back to the piano and pressed on the soft pedal. Her fingers drifted over the keys, playing a gentle lullaby on the highest octaves. She closed her eyes, a smile flickering as she composed new clauses. Eventually, her back began to ache and her toes grew numb from the chill. Drawing the song to a close, Adelia stood.

Clap.

Clap.

Clap.

The unmistakable sound of applause reverberated around the room.

The lid of the piano slammed down with a *snap* as Adelia looked around wildly for the culprit. Only shadows met her gaze. She fled.

Her heart pounded as she raced back through the house and up the stairs, the notion of staying quiet forgotten in her terror. On the landing, she leaned against the wall beneath the chandelier, grateful for its shadow-banishing light. The tension in her muscles began to ease as she gulped in mouthfuls of air. A mirror on the opposite wall reflected her pale, skinny form; dark hair a mess of curling rags and eyes wide orbs.

Slowly, reason started to catch up with her; she had been ridiculous. Quite clearly, there had been someone hiding behind the curtains. Most likely a servant trying to scare her. Possibly, it had been one of her father's important friends. There was a chance, she realised, that they had heard her song and come into the room without her noticing; she had been so wrapped up in the music. Of course, the claps hadn't sounded muffled, as they should have done if the applauder had been concealed behind the thick drapery of the velvet curtains. They had sounded as if someone was standing right behind her… Adelia shook her head abruptly. It was the only explanation, and that was that. Her wits returned, she began making her way back towards her room.

Then she noticed the blood.

Smeared at irregular intervals along the wood-panelled walls, it led all the way back down the staircase, drops glistening on the floor. Adelia's breath caught in her throat. Reaching out to a portrait of a stern-faced ancestor, she touched a splatter of the red liquid on the frame. Wet – and fresh. Without pausing to think, Adelia rushed to her bedroom and shook her mother awake.

"Quick, someone's hurt!" she cried, as her mother's eyes opened blearily.

"What are you talking about?" asked her mother, her sleep-thick words coloured with annoyance.

"There's blood! Lots of blood," said Adelia as – finally – her mother begrudgingly rose from the bed and allowed herself to be dragged out onto the landing.

"Look!" said Adelia, brandishing a hand in the direction of the blood-splattered portrait. Her mother frowned and Adelia followed her gaze. Where there had been smears of red only moments before, there was nothing.

"I-I don't understand," Adelia stuttered.

"Adelia," said her mother sharply. "You were dreaming again!"

"But I wasn't," the girl insisted, deciding to tell the truth. "I went downstairs to play the piano, then somebody started clapping so I got frightened and ran back upstairs. The landing was covered in blood. I swear it!"

"Don't be ridiculous," her mother said. "It was probably one of the hounds bringing in a rabbit, or perhaps Dotty cut her finger sewing again. One of the servants must have cleaned it up – if it wasn't just a figment of your overactive imagination. And why on earth did you go downstairs to play the piano in the first place, you could have woken the whole house? This is not the behaviour of a young lady, Adelia."

"But—"

"Enough!" her mother tugged her back into the bedroom, before releasing her and walking round to the far side of the bed.

"If you cannot sleep without screaming, nor wake without becoming hysterical there is little I can suggest – but kindly refrain from disturbing *my* night's rest."

Adelia lay awake, watching the grey light of dawn spread across the ceiling. The blood had been too high on the wall to be one of the dogs tugging it its mauled prize, and there was far too much for it to be from Dotty's pricked finger. Besides, no servant could have cleaned up the mess so quickly. The flood of light as Dotty flung open the curtains a couple of hours later was a welcome sight.

Around the breakfast table, most of her father's guests were already gathered, plates piled high. They rose politely when Adelia, her governess and her mother entered, then went back to ignoring them, their conversation raucous. This morning's topic – the victorious war. It was funny, Adelia thought, she had spent many hours concealed behind doors listening in to the servants' conversations and they never mentioned the Great War anymore, let alone discussed it. During the four long years when the men had been away, it was all the maids could talk about – fretting over absent brothers, fathers and the missing male household staff. Yet, when they returned, haunted, shadowed and reduced by half their numbers, Adelia never heard another word spoken of the event. She saw the effects though, in their footman Jack's startled eyes, in their gardener William's shaking hands, in the sobs of Lily the kitchen maid whose husband never made it home.

And yet these men – her father's friends – revelled in discussing battles won and victories gained. Adelia suspected that they'd had little to do with any of them.

"Tell the story of the Fritz who invaded your trench," bellowed one of them now, thrusting his fork at General Bullingdon. With a tight smile, Bullingdon pushed the fork away from his face.

"I think I've told that one enough times," he said. "Besides, it is hardly a story for the ladies' ears."

He nodded towards Adelia and her mother. Adelia frowned as she noticed the purple crescents beneath the general's eyes and his tired, sallow skin.

"Poppycock!" said the fork bearer, refusing to back down. "Tell the tale!"

Bullingdon cleared his throat, smoothing his napkin on the table.

"It was the last big push," he said. "I was visiting my men in the trenches, offering them support and showing them that I would fight alongside them if that was what king and country needed. I was taking a last look at the battle plans when Fritz burst into my quarters, gun trained on my heart. Naturally, I was a little alarmed–" the other men chuckled appreciatively– "he had caught me off guard."

"But, quick as a flash, you grabbed your rifle and fired!" crowed another of the men.

Bullingdon nodded. "Quite so, I fired two shots and both hit their mark."

The fork-bearer used the utensil to point at his heart and head, sticking his tongue out in a grotesque impression of the dead German soldier.

"First and last time you visited the trenches, eh, Bullingdon?" piped up her father, his wheedling voice wiping the smile off Bullingdon's face.

"And how many times did you visit the front line, Adams?" Bullingdon whipped back.

Adelia's father bowed his head deferentially, spots of pink appearing high on his cheeks. The footmen entered and began gathering up the plates. A crash of china brought the conversation to an abrupt halt. Adelia glanced up to see Jack, a tea tray flipped in his hands, watching Bullingdon with a glare as steely as the December sky. Recovering himself, the young man apologised and scooped up the broken crockery. The butler cuffed Jack around the back of the head. The whole episode lasted little more than a few seconds, and soon the men returned to their conversation, but Adelia's gaze remained fixed firmly on the spot that Jack had absented.

At the earliest opportunity she excused herself and surreptitiously made her way to the servants' quarters. A familiar silhouette sat hunched on the bottom step, shining her father's shoes.

"Jack?" she said quietly.

The young man leapt up, his hands flinching to cover his head. Slowly he lowered his arms and cleared his throat awkwardly. Adelia admonished herself for startling him, but it was difficult not to. The footman's tendency to flinch at the slightest noise was what had earned him the nickname 'Jumpy Jack'.

"Do you know if anyone was hurt last night? I saw blood upstairs," she asked. If one of the servants knew about it, they all would.

Jack shook his head. "No, Miss Adams. Perhaps one of the dogs?"

Adelia frowned. So nobody else had seen it. How was that possible? Perhaps her mother was right, and somehow she had dreamt the whole event. Unless…

"You don't know if … was anyone watching me play the piano, in the middle of the night? I thought I heard – something. I won't be cross," she added quickly.

Again, Jack shook his head. "I shouldn't think so, Miss Adams. Everyone was exhausted from the celebrations, they wouldn't have risen before they had to."

"Of course," said Adelia, her mind reeling. "Did you enjoy the fireworks?"

Jack bowed his head. "To be honest, Miss, I stayed below. The bangs—"

He cut himself off and kept his eyes firmly fixed on the ground. Adelia reddened.

"Thank you," she said, turning to go. But something made her look back. "Do you … know General Bullingdon?" she asked.

The footman's eyes narrowed and Adelia saw his hands twitch into fists.

"Yes, Miss. He visited my regiment, toward the end of the war."

Adelia could see that he was holding himself back from saying anything further. Instinctively, Adelia reached out a hand to touch his arm.

"Tell me," she whispered, as Jack's haunted eyes flicked to hers.

"I had a mate, Harry Townson. We were waiting to go over the top together, when the lieutenant asked him to deliver a message to General Bullingdon. The telephones were down, you see. Harry set off back through the trenches. But according to Bullingdon, the message never arrived. Instead, he swore he saw Harry running away from the front line. Deserting."

Jack's breathing became ragged as he recalled the tale.

"Harry was no deserter. He was one of the best of us. Sang stupid songs to keep the young'uns from going mad as the shells shattered right above our heads – loved music, see? I'll be damned if Bullingdon's story has an ounce of truth in it. He told us that a German had got a bullet in Harry's back as he ran."

He took a steadying breath then took a step backwards, increasing the distance between Adelia and himself.

"You should go upstairs, Miss. You don't want Governess to catch you down here."

Adelia nodded, though she wished she could stay. She'd always felt more at home among the clashes and clangs of the kitchen, than the stuffy silence of the upper floors.

Puzzling over Jack's words, she set off back up the stairs. The men were gathered by the front door, off to survey the ground in a flurry of swishing coats. Her shoulders prickled again and she squeezed her eyes closed for a beat, willing herself to stay calm. Outside her mother's room, she paused. This was where the general was sleeping. Guiltily, she pushed the door open and stepped inside.

A pile of clothes lay in a chest at the bottom of the bed, and a comb and tobacco box were on the dresser. Adelia made her way over to the dresser, lightly touching each object. She glanced up at the mirror and her heart stopped. Reflected in the glass, was a German soldier. A dark stain spread across his shoulder and chest, his uniform splattered with thick blood. Worse still, the top half of the left side of his face was missing, the skull glinting through a mess of pink, stringy flesh. Great globs of blood fell from the wounds onto the carpet below, pooling at his feet. A scent – metallic and sickly – wafted through the air. Wearing the grey overcoat and spiked helmet she recognised from propaganda posters, the soldier reached his hand towards her.

Adelia shrieked and span around.

There was nothing there. But a hint of that terrible smell lingered.

Where was the soldier?

Swallowing down a sob, she raced from the room.

Adelia spent the rest of the afternoon trailing first her mother, then her governess. Usually so keen to avoid them, both were brimming with questions as to what was wrong. Adelia kept quiet, the image of the bloody soldier returning again and again, as if he were right in front of her. Dinner came around and Adelia could barely look at her food, let alone eat it. She tried to catch Jack's eye, the only person she felt might just believe what she had seen, may even have an explanation for it, but he looked determinedly away.

After dinner was over, the whole party gathered in the games room. Cards were laid and her father brought out the best brandy, still hoping that the weekend would prove fruitful for business investments. Adelia sat, pale and silent, a book open in her lap. What had General Bullingdon brought into their home? The more she thought about it, the more convinced she became that the phantom in the mirror was real. First the terror in the night, then the ghostly clapping, the blood on the landing…

The sickly smell of metal and flesh washed over her.

A short gasp from the other side of the room; General Bullingdon's gaze was fixed on a point near the bookshelves. Following his eyeline, Adelia saw the soldier step out of the shadows. He raised a bloodied hand and pointed at the general. Adelia met General Bullingdon's gaze. For a beat, the world stood still as she stared at his terrified eyes, the injured soldier in her periphery. The general looked away.

"Excuse me," he apologised to the room. "I twinged an old wound. I shall go and tend to it."

He set off towards the door, but paused beside Adelia, pretending to adjust a buckle on his shoe.

"You see him?" he hissed, so quietly Adelia had to lean in to hear.

She nodded minutely. "Yes."

"After a moment, follow me," he whispered.

With an unsteady gait, the general left the room. Adelia watched as the soldier followed, somehow unseen by the rest of the party. She held her breath as he passed by her. Slowly, Adelia stood and bid the party goodnight, rushing from the room so hastily, she almost tripped over Jack on his way in with the port.

Adelia didn't need to dither over which direction the general had headed. The soldier's blood led the way through the house until she reached the entrance to the roof terrace. Clambering up the narrow stairs, she found herself blinking in the starlight, the white stone of the roof rendered ethereal in the glow. On the parapet, General Bullingdon sat, head in his hands, the soldier standing over him silently. Unlike the ghostly illustrations of spirits in her books, the soldier looked solid, the crimson blood vibrant. The only hint of his spectral nature was the silvery glow surrounding him – and that his injuries were hardly sustainable with life.

"You see him now?" the general croaked.

"Yes," Adelia said again. "He's standing over you."

"He's been following me since the end of the war," the general said, looking up at her. Adelia was horrified to see his eyes glistening with tears. "It's unbearable."

Adelia glanced at the soldier, telling herself not to be afraid. An overwhelming sense of sadness flooded through her as the soldier's good eye met hers, but she felt no malice.

"But, why doe he follow you?" she puzzled aloud. "Thousands of soldiers died. If every Englishman was haunted by the Germans he killed, there would be a trail of ghostly figures behind every man."

"Unless he is not a German soldier," said a voice from behind Adelia, startling her so much that she stumbled. Jack took her arm, steadying her.

The general looked at the footman, and Adelia thought she saw a new kind of fear dancing in her eyes.

"Don't worry," Jack said to her. "I followed you – I believe in your ghost. What does he look like?"

"He's wearing a German uniform," said Adelia, confused.

"Yes, but beyond that," Jack said, moving towards the spot that Adelia and the general kept glancing at. The German didn't look up, as if he couldn't see the man nearly treading on his toes.

"He has brown hair and his eye is blue." Adelia paused as the soldier reached into his pocket and held out an envelope with a name scrawled on the front. She gasped. "He has a message, addressed to the general."

"Harry," Jack breathed. "It's you, isn't it?"

The ghostly soldier frowned, as if trying to remember something from a very long time ago.

"I don't understand," Adelia said, as Jack reached out, trying to grasp hold of his invisible comrade. "I thought that this soldier was the Fritz from the general's story, the one who attacked him in the trench."

"They are one and the same," Jack said, his teeth grinding together to contain his anger. "Think, Miss Adams. How could the general beat a soldier whose gun was already drawn? And how could a German make it back through our trenches – unhindered – to surprise him in the first place?"

The general cleared his throat. "You have to understand what it was like," he said in a high voice. "The bangs, the crashes – I couldn't bear it! And then this private burst into my room unannounced – how was I supposed to know he was delivering a message? Naturally I thought he was a Fritz! So yes, I shot him."

Jack rounded on him, tugging the general up by his collar. "Even that – cowardly and thoughtless though it was – could have been forgiven. But what you did next—"

"I have my reputation!" roared the general. "And the men's morale! Just as we were about to go over the top, what would they think if they knew a general had shot one of their own?"

"So you took one of the enemies' uniforms from the stores, and dressed Harry's corpse, so nobody would know what you'd done," said Jack, shoving his superior back against the parapet. "You turned yourself into a hero, and made

Harry into a villain twice over. He was the German soldier who attacked you *and* the deserter you watched abandon his companions."

Adelia blinked, absorbing the full horror of the tale. "You dishonoured his memory by telling his friends and family that he ran away."

"And dishonoured his body by leaving him to be buried with his enemies rather than his friends," growled Jack. "No wonder he haunts you."

"Yes," said the general, all the fight gone out of him. "I am guilty. But I have paid the price – for two long years. I will confess, if it means this phantom will leave me, I swear it"

The soldier sighed deeply. He gave a smile so peaceful it transformed his maimed face. He reached a hand out to the general, as if to shake it, but misreading the gesture General Bullingdon scrambled backwards, and tumbled over the parapet. For an impossible moment, he fell. The three of them watched, helpless as the body cracked on the gravel below.

The silence that followed was notably absent of sobs or gasps. For Jack and Harry, too many worthier men had gone unmourned. For Adelia, shock was present, and horror too, but no sadness.

The soldier turned and headed back down the stairs.

"He's gone," Adelia told Jack. The footman nodded once and swallowed.

A few moments later, the soldier began walking down the drive. He spared no glance for the broken body on the floor, nor his friend on the roof.

"He's heading towards the gate," she said. "Where do you think he's going?"

"To lie down with his brothers," replied Jack. "Come, we shouldn't be up here. Someone will find the body soon enough."

Together they walked quickly and quietly back through the house. Laughter came from the drawing room, where the men were still at their games.

Adelia stopped suddenly. "Now the general is dead, no one will know the truth of Harry's story! Nobody will believe us!"

Jack nodded slowly. "You're right. But they might believe your father…"

With that, he set off towards the drawing room and his duties. Adelia frowned – her father was the least likely to listen to, let alone accept, a tale of phantom soldiers and corruption. Even if he did, he'd be too fearful of the repercussions to condemn the actions of a respected general. What had Jack meant…?

The answer struck like a bolt of lightning from the sky.

*

Adelia didn't know what made the newspaper decide to print the letter. It had been a long shot, really. But gossip over General Bullingdon's suicide was rife, and the editors had seized on this scandalous explanation of a guilt-ridden traitor haunted by his dishonourable deception. Besides,

Mr Adams was reputable enough, and the letter bore his signature. The public accepted the explanation of foul play because it was just the sort of behaviour they had come to expect of the aristocracy. Mr Adams swore blind the letter was forged, but his former friends were doubtful – it was in such bad taste that of course he would deny it. Did Adelia feel any guilt for marring not only the reputation of the general, but also her father? Perhaps a little. But somehow, she felt the soldier had chosen her to carry the truth, and she had accepted the burden. She hoped that somewhere, he was at peace.

Call Me Autumn

by Mark Gibson

(3rd Place)

It has become my habit, on a fair evening with an ebb tide and when the wind is nothing but a gentle kiss from the south, to sit on the old bench by the Ness of Duncansby and watch the boats go by and the sun set slowly behind the Island of Stroma. Long have I done this and I hope I long shall, but one incident, just this last year, is an illustration of the interesting situations that can arise from so simple a pleasure.

I was on the seat as usual. Behind me the breeze blew but it had an autumnal air, for the year had turned again, as all years do, over and over in the endless cycle of the seasons. Before me the sea shimmered under the lowering sun, occasionally hiding behind a wispy grey cloud. I felt the chill and drew more closer around me the old brown coat that I invariably wear. I used to think that I would miss that coat when it wore out. Comfortable in familiarity it enveloped and hugged me like and old friend rather than merely sheltered me from the elements. But I do not fear that loss now. Everything and everyone must die and when we do, coat or winding sheet, it matters not what we wear. Death is a leveller in all things fashionable.

But I was not there to think of death. When I sit on that seat it is life that breathes through me. The scent of the sea; a heady aroma for a sailor like me. I keenly smelled the air and watched the waves rolling and playing and topping each other like little children free from the constraints of the big wide ocean, but then to dash themselves on the rocks and shoals. But it was not really a death. There they are again. Running and rolling out on the Firth again to play the same risky game, every time to be reborn and be mirthful once more. I know those little waves can kill as well as their larger parents and have a healthy respect for them, but I love to see them.

And the sun. Oh the sun in its glorious progress, now autumnal and low,

heading down to be swallowed by the sea between St John's Point and the majestic Hoy. Big golden orb turning burnished brass. Stately progress in an ever tightening arc sweeping down below the horizon a little earlier each day and rising just a little later. The journey through the underworld just a little bit longer. First flush of summer long gone and heat burned out on green ground and purple heather.

With a start – yes a genuine start – I realised that someone was sitting next to me. I had neither seen or heard or even felt her approach. How she got there I did not know. It was as if she had been conjured by the playful waves and the falling sun as a way of breaking my reverie.

I turned to look at her. I am a forward man, always was. A true sailor knows death may come visit him with the next wave or the next tide and that time is not here to be wasted.

She was a pale slim thing. Very pale, her skin almost seemed to my rheumy eyes diaphanous, like the thinnest and most delicate of parchments. She had ash blonde hair which flowed like a mane down her back and around her shoulders and her hands had long fingers with red painted nails, a high gloss to the generally matt finish of the rest of her. Her forehead was high and her lips thin but her eyes were big and green and wild and were the only thing that made me think she had animation and life.

Her clothing was simple and practical. She wore grey flat shoes and pale cream tights and a knee length tweed skirt with a white blouse and waist length grey almost formless raincoat over the rest. It was not the fashion for a young woman but she was not old. I considered her age. Thirty perhaps? Or a young forty. Who knows the mysteries of pinpointing the vintages of women. Some are old before their time like a corked wine. Others are still bubbly and fresh after long in the bottle. You have to taste to really know.

I smiled at her and she smiled a thin smile back. But if she had not wanted a conversation I doubted she would have come to share my bench. There were plenty of nice flat rocks by the beach.

“A pleasant evening.”

“The weather. Ah. Always a safe conversation starter.” Her voice was initially crisp but I sensed a warmth in it deep down. An amusement there which belied the sarcastic tone. An old violin rather than an upright piano. But there also seemed to be a sadness. Perhaps I was reading too much. I do sometimes.

“The weather is important here. It can mean the difference between life and death. Ach but that is a heavy subject for such a calm evening. My name is Davy.”

I held out my hand to her. She paused for a moment and then took it. It felt cold, like a beached fish. Her grip was slight and she let go quickly, as if receiving a shock from my gnarled paw.

“You have a name I suppose?”

“Call me Autumn”

I felt the wind increase at my back and a tingle play Greig down my spine. Autumn. Autumn. It is a falsehood that April is cruel. At least there is the promise of a summer. Autumn has warmth but no promise except that of a future long and dark before the Spring comes again.

“Autumn is an apt name today.”

“It was almost Summer, but I was born late.”

“American names? Or at least more used in America. You have connections there?”

She stroked her hair back from her eyes where the wind had flicked it. It was a simple movement done gracefully.

“My mother was from San Francisco. Bit of a hippy. Not something I was ever into much. I was a daddy's girl.”

“What work do you do?”

“Nothing. Now.”

Silence for a while. Then she turned back the question.

“What work do you do?

I smiled and stared at my scuffed boots. “Like you, nothing now. But I worked on boats most of my life.”

“You left that work? You do not look old. I thought that the sea gets into your blood?”

I smiled to myself. “The sea does get into the blood but she is also a cruel mistress. Dangerous and cruel.”

I changed the subject.

“What brings you here Autumn?”

She stared out at the sea. It was a long stare but her eyes were full of

longing.

“Peace. We all want peace I suppose.” She paused a little. Caught her breath, wondered perhaps if she could or would say more. I let her fight her own emotions; decide for herself. I kept my own peace and stillness. Stillness is often all that people need to gain the courage to say things.

“I had a man and he was not a good man and then I lost him.”

“Is a tainted thing a bad loss?”

She smiled sadly. “It seems sometimes as if it is. I suppose it feels like that because of the loneliness. It was a bad marriage but I was with someone. Now I am not.”

We both stared out at the sea for a while; as if the gentle breaking of the waves and the setting of the sun were a balm to soothe past hurt.

I asked gently “was it your decision to be alone?”

She shook her head and held her hands tightly together in her lap. Her skin looked even more fragile. “No. Death separated us.”

I shook my own head. “I am sorry. Death has a way of doing that. I have

had my own fill of it.”

“Not as much as me. “ She wrung her hands. “We fought a lot. Argued all the time. He did nothing right and neither did I. There were no children to keep us together but still we remained, terrible twins locked in a long hated embrace.

“It was I suppose inevitable. That one or the other of us would take their life. A huge game of Russian roulette with the loser left lying on a bed with a bottle of gin and an empty tablet bottle.”

The chill I felt deepened just as the sun deepened to red as it neared the water and the sunk began to creep in around us. The warmth of the day leached into the earth like the seeping blood from a jagged wound.

And then I wondered. Tablets seemed like a female way to me. I know there is no discrimination in death but I also had an idea that for some twisted reasons most men tended to choose more violent deaths.

I stared sidelong at this strange woman sat beside me and I wondered.

Now I am not afraid of the other world. The world beyond the veil. There is much more to fear, believe me, on the living side of the equation. But deep inside me was a growing realisation that this situation was somewhat amiss.

I began to wonder who or what sat next to me on that bench in the far North of Scotland, staring out at Orkney on an Autumn evening. It was a mad thought of course. Not because I do not believe in ghosts, I know they exist; but because I also believe in other things, less friendly entities; and I was beginning to wonder ….

Something, some shadow, must have shown in my face. She turned to face me again, those large eyes now disturbingly alluring, deep as green water.

“Is something disturbing you? Did my talk of death upset you?”

I decided to be honest. If she was supernatural then it was best to face that fact. If she was not then it was a moments embarrassment.

“I did begin to wonder where you were from. Up here in this part of the world we have many tales and many superstitions. Not all of them can be easily dismissed.”

She laughed. It was a warm sound now. The land breathing after a thaw.

“I am stopping at the caravan site! Where did you think I was from? I stay in Glasgow, but well, after my husband killed himself I needed to get away.”

I was disappointed I suppose, but tried not to show it. This was not a Gothic tale but just one of a sad girl from down South on a personal voyage of discovery or escape. No succubus was about to take me, though I would have been very lean meat for one.

“I wondered for a while, that you might not be of this earth.”

She looked at me, a little startled.

"You thought I had been the one to die?! You thought I was a ghost!?"

I smiled back and glanced out to the ocean again, where the sun now had half her dome under the water.

"No, not a ghost as such. Perhaps a personification. You see, I think I know what ghosts are like."

She gave me a little amused smile back, as if not really believing me. "You know ghosts do you? Care to tell me how?"

Anxiously I looked at the sun again. Almost gone. When she hits the sea she moves quick.

I turned to face Autumn and pointed out to end of Stroma where white water churned.

"Do you see that? The white water there?"

She nodded. Still the amused smile on her face. It made her look beautiful at last, and very alive. It pulled at my heart. The sun now was lost beneath the waves. Drowned. I felt it. Felt it tug. Not long now.

"Out there, only three fathoms down lie the bones of a boat and in it are the bones of a man in an old brown coat. Out there are *my* bones, whitened by sea."

But I had not time to explain because the weeds were drawing me back now, as they always do and have done for over sixty years, and the sound of the sea was loud in my ears and my sight dimmed green. I felt the eddy and cold and the dampness and knew my physical form was fading to nothing.

I knew this because I saw the horror in her eyes, all her beauty gone now in the terror of what she had just witnessed.

But I will be back, on a fair evening with a ebb tide and when the wind is nothing but a gentle kiss from the south, to sit on the old bench by the Ness of Duncansby and watch the boats go by and the sun set slowly behind the Island of Stroma. Long have I done this and long shall I until my bones pull apart and are spread by the tides.

So the next time you sit on that seat, take note of who you sit with. It might just be me.

I'll Wait for You

by Ellen Evers

The light is dim but I can make out her shape in the corner, feet curled under her in a way I know so well. The drugs have mercifully kicked in and I'm in that euphoric daze that unfortunately lasts no time at all. The nurse must sense my awareness and offers the straw, welcome water and a soothing face wipe.

Carys appears at the bed side. As usual the smell of the sea envelops her - the sharp tang of seaweed - I can almost taste the brine. She is dressed as always in the pink ruched bathing costume she loved. I can see the freckles, the long brown limbs, and the heavy wet plait that hangs over her shoulder.

My little sister, dead these fifty years.

The drug haze lifts and I allow myself to remember.

After the tragedy, the farm became a shrine to Carys; her photographs dominated every room. Lest we forget, as if we could. It was a constant reminder to those left that she was the best, brightest, and most perfect of all creatures – an angel in every way. She was everything I wasn't – I take after Dad's Welsh stock; dark, short, and fierce whilst my sister had the beauty of some English ancestor of Mam's.

It didn't end there; she was as pleasant as a summer's day. Even our brothers treated her kindly and looked out for her. Nothing riled her or made her cross. Not even me, and by God I tried. She worshipped me. I was her big sister and could do no wrong. It was my job to look after her and I'd failed. Guilt overwhelmed grief.

Afterwards I flung myself into school work, chores around the farm, helping Mam and Dad through their loss trying desperately to ignore the fact that my sister in death was the presence she'd been in life. I saw her as clearly as I saw Mam sobbing, just as I'd seen her on that very last day. I couldn't tell anyone - who'd believe me?

The funeral at our Methodist chapel was something they talked about for years after. All the children from school came and our headmaster read out the eulogy – no-one in the family could do it. I sat at the front in my thick black Sunday coat despite the heat and she perched on the step to the pulpit looking right back at me. When she held her arms aloft in the way she had done when she was a little girl wanting to be picked up, I fainted and had to be taken out, emotion and heat blamed.

Unsurprisingly, this was making me ill and Mam took a break from her mourning to take me to the doctors where I was prescribed a tonic for my nerves. Carys sat in the surgery, smiling with a sweet sadness and twirling the end of her plait in the way that always drove me mad. That was the first time I noticed the smell of the sea.

Rather bizarrely, it became the norm. On the way to school I'd find myself chatting to her about the plans I'd made, almost forgetting who I was talking to. Then she'd fix her big brown doleful eyes on me and the realisation that there would be no plans for her would hit me. I'd fall into guilty silence.

She sat in her usual place in the parlour in the evening and when I went to bed she would follow; sitting, feet curled on the window seat, there while I slept, there when I woke. She sat as I studied, sat as I grew, as I aged, as she did not.

The first Christmas after was the worst. Mam and Dad carried on as if Carys was there and of course she was, as far I was concerned. They laid a place for her at Christmas dinner, an empty chair ,but I could see her , dripping her plait and smiling while we all wept.

There were even presents under the tree, all wrapped and labelled. We took it in turns to open one for our sister. When I revealed the bathing costume Mam had made me wrap I couldn't take any more and escaped to my room. From that Christmas onwards, the season was never anything but misery to me . We always set a place for Carys.

My escape was university. She would disappear , I was sure, as I felt that somehow, she was grounded in the farm, our home. What I based that on I don't know having no knowledge of such things but spirits haunt places don't they?

I clung to Mam as they said goodbye outside the Hall of Residence, Dad uncomfortable and anxious to be gone. I was excited and scared at the big adventure ahead. For a while Carys was not on my mind, that is until I opened the door of my room and found her sitting on my bed, smiling and twirling the plait. Ghosts haunted people I soon realised.

The three years away passed. I worked hard on the science that would help the farm. Carys was at my side, saying nothing but looking reproachfully with those big brown eyes. Having boyfriends became a nightmare and any kind of intimacy impossible so I just didn't bother, it was easier that way.

I returned to the farm full of plans for the future much against Dad's better judgement and my brothers' old - fashioned ideas. It was a struggle but it paid off. Mam and Dad moved to a bungalow where boredom sent them dementia bound to a care home.

It was a lonely life. My brothers, tired of Welsh farming moved away and started families of their own and they became my surrogate children. My nephews and nieces spent every Christmas at the farm and heard the story of Carys, gazing with intent concentration at the photographs, many still in the same place as Mam had placed them long before. I think they liked the spookiness of the empty chair which we continued as a Christmas tradition.

They begged me to tell the story of Carys. Ignorance was my defence; I pretended I did not know why Carys swam out to Grymnor rocks when we had been banned. It was long ago I would say. Carys sat, smiling and twirling, listening to my stuttered explanations and nodding with approval at the photos and the empty place. I didn't tell the truth. How could I?

As is the way, the children grew up, grew away from me, losing interest in the farm that I fought to keep solvent. They kept in touch but the visits became less frequent and I found myself talking more and more to Carys like some batty old woman. She listened and smiled her sweet smile but stayed silent.

Dad died quite suddenly but Mam with the resilience of the old kept a tight grip on life. The dementia had changed her, not for the better, and now she would say all the things that she had only thought all those years before.

'Why wasn't it you Gwyneth? Your Dad cried every night after she went, she was our baby,' she would sob and pluck the sheets, 'you should have taken better care of her. It's your fault we lost her. You thought more about yourself…always were a selfish bitch… 'until I could stand no more and had to go out.

Carys would stand in the shadows listening to our Mam's distress. After one particularly horrible visit, Mam sat up in bed looked directly at Carys, eyes wide, pupils dilated and then she began to scream with such anguish that I decided that I would not visit again.

All this I remember as the drugs do their work and Carys stays close knowing as I do that my time is short. The smell of the sea grows stronger. The past envelops me.

The hot summer of 1963 - the busy harvest and long evenings when everyone worked to bring in the hay. We were tired and scratchy with the drudgery; the sun had burned my skin sore and red but Carys had the golden hue of a beautiful blond.

'Let's swim. They won't miss us.' I said, lying on the hay rick, bored, edgy, wishing myself anywhere but here. Ivor from the village had said some would be meeting up at the beach. I sighed, impatient that Carys would have to string along. Why did she have to come everywhere with me? The others used to mock, 'Here comes me and my shadow'. Nobody else had to drag their kid sister around. I felt mulish as we made our way back to the house to change into swimming gear.

She was so excited I remember as she struggled into the pink bathing costume that was her favourite, pulling on her shorts and eager to get going. The beach was close, down the steep path to the rocks; an easy walk and scramble and I could see Ivor and some others waiting for me. Rushing down the track with Carys calling, 'Wait for me Gwyn!' like some irritating puppy I didn't look back. Mam didn't think Ivor was good enough coming from the village; she thought him common. My sister was bound to say something – she had no guile.

How was I to shake Carys off?

I reached the beach breathless and somehow the glint of the sun on Grymnor Rocks gave me the idea. By the time Carys had slithered next to me I knew what I would do.

'Let's swim to Grymnor. You go first and I'll watch you and catch up and we'll get to the rocks together.'

Carys shielded her eyes from the sun's glare. 'But Gwyn, we're not allowed. You know Dad warned us about the currents.'

I mimicked her.

'But Gwyn we're not allowed…honestly Carys, you are such a drip. You want to swim but you don't want to improve.'

Carys gnawed her lip. 'You know I'm not as good as you at swimming.'

I snorted. 'Well here's your chance to get better. I'll be right behind you. It'll be fine. Be more adventurous.' She gave me her trembly - mouthed smile.

'I'll try really hard Gwyn, you'll see – you'll be proud.' With that she took a gangly lope across the beach, waded into the water shouting, 'I'll wait for you!'

I watched her ungainly stroke as she managed the waves. She'd be ages. I'd quickly make up the difference and have time to see Ivor briefly.

I must have done but I have only a vague memory of furtive fumbling and wet kisses. The next thing I remember is someone shouting that there was a swimmer on Grymnor Rocks, someone in a pink costume, someone waving…

Then nothing. She just disappeared.

I ran back to get Dad and help but too late. Despite everyone's effort we couldn't find her. Stronger swimmers than me tried by swimming through the currents, Dad first and fastest. But she'd gone.

Her body was washed up the next day.

And now so many years on, she stands as young and fresh as she ever was, with a tremulous smile, twirling the plait and with the voice of the sea whispers,

'I waited for you, Gwyn, just as I promised…'

The Ghost in the Mansion

by Daniel Metcalfe

(Children's Runner-Up)

Guns blasting, the British forces were diminished by Germans. Enemies and allies were falling to the ground like puppets who had just lost their strings. The British were slowly falling back, yet their enemies kept coming as if there was no end to their army. The remaining soldiers cowered behind a devastated tank - they all knew that it would only be a matter of time.

It had all started a week ago when the Inferno squadron had been briefed on their last mission that would end the war; which had cost millions of lives of both civilians and soldiers. At that time, it all seemed so simple, as simple as firing the artillery. It had only been a few minutes ago that they had received a transmission saying that they had intercepted one of the enemies' Morse code messages. The Germans had backup!

Back in the present, private Ryan had spotted a trail leading into the forest. Swiftly the squadron ran into the undergrowth. After a couple of minutes of running, stumbling, tripping and falling they were sure that they had put enough distance between them and the Germans, then they stopped for a well-deserved rest. They tried to contact base command but there was some interference. Out of the canopy, they could see something that looked like a mansion with its giant window, pointed spires and large balconies. Tangled vines entwined the house as if they were part of the structure itself. They hesitated deciding something. Was it inhabited?!

After several minutes they thought from the state of the house itself that it was not inhabited. They sent a search party of 3 of the 10 men in Inferno squad into the building. The search party had found some comfy beds, slightly out of date food and some ammunition to replenish their supplies.

Night was falling fast and after an intense day the men sent one person out to the spire window to be a lookout. In the early hours the team were awakened by a loud and terrified scream. Private Ryan had found a dead body where the lookout should have been and for some strange reason he had chalk white hair and pale skin, as if all of the life had been sucked out of him!

The next morning, the weather was quite dismal. The rain battered down as if the sky hurled rocks down at them. From then on, they decided that whenever they needed to go somewhere they needed to go in pairs or threes. They realised that the thing that killed the lookout could still be nearby so they went on a hunt for it. They expected to find a German spy but they found nothing: no footprints, no signs, nothing. It was if it didn't even exist. They had another look round the house. This time they found a note with a red stain on it, it said:

'I am the last one left it has taken them all. It comes at night even if you stick together it manages to get you. It takes one of you per night, you can't attack it. Whatever you do to protect yourself will fail, it just passes right through it. If you are reading this it is coming for you. I tried the doors they are locked. Oh no it is coming, it always knows where I am. These may be the last words I get a chance to write. Save yourself!'

As the note had said the doors where jammed. A moment of terror passed through them all, the person was right they were already dead!

It was the second night and the tensions were high, for the first time they thought being together was dangerous. It was spine-chilling knowing that this night one of them would not be in this world for much longer.

That was eight nights ago, now Private Ryan was all by himself and he had seen it. Seen the Spectre that had patrolled the house like a policeman guarding the prisoners. He had seen the horrible ways of torture as he and the others stood and watched and sadly could not help the victim. Not even bullets couldn't penetrate its ghostly skin. When it had locked on to its chosen victim, it would hunt him down without even glancing back at the others. As soon as he was captured, it would start (what looked like) sucking out his soul! Private Ryan sneaked about the house, he was light on his feet trying to avoid attention from his killer. The house was silent. He had no way of knowing where it was, that was when he saw the door. His heart skipped a beat, but something was nagging at him as if he had forgotten something. Suddenly the temperature dropped, he could see frost on the inside of the window. All of the hairs on the back of his neck stood on end. Slowly he turned around, metres away was a bright light that was begging him to come closer. Then, it flickered off then back on, but then he noticed something that happened. Each time it flickered off he saw a misty veil surrounding a human like figure - only there was one unnatural thing about it. Its body floated inches above the ground like a puppet on a string!

The light came and stayed on and he knew it could be anywhere even right in front of him! He spun around now he only had a couple of minutes maybe even thirty seconds until he would fall to the ground as if his bones were jelly. He tried to open the doors but still they were locked. Ryan glanced back but as he did he regretted it, the monster was a couple of feet away and knew he had no chance of leaving this horror house. Private Ryan was suddenly lifted into the air and was turned around only to come face to face with it!

The creature had the face of an old woman. Although she had long silky hair, it could not hide her true self; in places skin was peeling away from her feeble bones like a horrible sunburn. He was full of pain and sadness as if nothing in the world could make him happy and in a few seconds it would all be over, all of his pain and suffering! As he fell to the ground, the doors swung open as if waiting for their next victims.

The Germans had spent days tracking the Inferno squadron. But they were so good, that it seemed as if the Inferno squadron had disappeared off the face of the earth. Soon they found a long-abandoned house that would be a great base camp. They were exhausted and needed to rest in a safe place. They felt that something was wrong but their eyes were heavy, and they were glad of a place to rest and work out where Inferno squadron had gone. Landser Schmidt picked up a piece of crumpled paper, and read the English words, as the doors shut behind them…

Christmas Presence

by Chris Palmer

The pain in his side was like nothing Robbie had ever felt before. It enveloped him in a bright white light, blotting out almost all of his vision.

Around the edges of the pain, Robbie was aware that he was lying down in something cold and wet. Judging by both the stench and the gritty texture he guessed it was mud. He had no more idea how he got there than how he got hurt. None of those details seemed important, dwarfed as they were by the pain.

He felt himself trying to sit up. The effort made him scream loud enough to frighten himself.

He was now able to get a better view of his surroundings. Marginally. The air was full of thick black smoke with a smell that faintly reminded Robbie of fireworks, but he could tell that it came from something meaner than rockets and roman candles. The ground was scarred and uneven without a hint of anything growing. He could see no more than three or four metres in any direction, which was fine by him. He did not want to know what lay beyond.

There was silence so profound it was deafening. Robbie tried to call out, but the sound died in his throat. He was terrified that whatever was hidden within the smoke would seek him out. Whatever lurked in that battered hellscape would mean him nothing but harm.

The footsteps were hard to identify at first. Thick, wet mud let out disgusting squelches which steadily grew louder. Someone was getting closer.

Robbie twisted his body, trying to look in all directions at the same time. The movement unleashed a new wave of white-hot pain, so intense that he nearly passed out before it subsided.

Still the footsteps came closer.

Robbie's left hand dropped instinctively to his waist. He felt his fingers close around something metallic and heavy. He raised what he was surprised to see was a loaded revolver. The weapon felt natural in his hand even as he stared incredulously at the first real gun he'd ever seen.

Robbie scanned the impossibly close horizon past the sights on his revolver, alert and ready for slightest hint of movement. He forced himself to breathe slowly, instinctively knowing this would improve his aim.

A hazy figure emerged from the smoke directly in front of him. He tried to call out a warning, but the words "Stop right there" came out wrong. The voice wasn't his voice and the words were alien to him.

The figure paused for a moment. It was close enough now for him to make out some details. It was a young man, not much older than Robbie himself. He wore similar clothes to Robbie, but there were subtle differences. Uniforms, but not the same uniform. This man was not on his side.

The other man started to raise his arms. Robbie couldn't be sure if he was surrendering or reaching for a weapon and he didn't want to find out. He squeezed the trigger.

Click.

Wide-eyed, Robbie tried again, each squeeze a little wilder than the last as the reality dawned.

Click. Click. Click.

Robbie turned the weapon over in his hands. It was coated with black mud.

In the moment his attention was distracted, the other man was on him. Even as he fell Robbie wondered why the other man didn't just shoot. Didn't he have a gun, too? Robbie reached out to grab his attacker by the throat, dimly aware as he did so of the torrent of blood gushing from his original wound.

It wasn't a fair fight. The other man was as desperate as him, but he was also uninjured. The strength drained from Robbie's arms even before he felt the cold steel of the knife pierce his chest.

The world around him span and faded to black. Even as his consciousness slipped away he had time to notice that the silence had now been broken by a familiar sound.

People were singing. He was losing a fight to the death and somewhere nearby someone was singing *Silent Night…*

#

Robbie sat bolt upright in bed and let out a high-pitched scream. His hands flew to his chest and side, searching for the wounds that only moments ago had seemed so real.

The pain was gone. The wounds were gone.

"Daddy!" He screamed again. He could hear a second scream from the adjoining room and even through his terror he recognised the voice of his older sister. She sounded scared, too.

It took only seconds for his parents to make it up the stairs. His father, Patrick, came to him while his mother, Joanna, tended to Jess.

Robbie wrapped himself in his father's powerful arms. Then the tears came, huge sobs that sent shudders through Robbie's whole being.

Gradually, the fear and disorientation left Robbie and he was able to tell his father all about what he now knew to have been a nightmare.

When he'd finished Robbie looked into his father's eyes, searching the for reassurance that he knew would come.

"Shhh… It was just a bad dream. We all get bad dreams sometimes."

“Even you, Daddy?” said Robbie.

“Even me,” said Patrick, nodding sadly. There was something strange about how Daddy said that.

Patrick blinked and took a quick breath.

“Anyway, it’s time you went back to sleep. It’s all over now. Nothing to be afraid of anymore. It’s Christmas Eve tomorrow. Only two sleeps to presents!”

“What if I have the dream again?”

“You won’t. I know you won’t”.

Robbie wished he could be so sure.

#

Robbie waited until both parents were back downstairs before he made his move. He slid his feet over the side of his bed and stood up. He inched out of his room, transferring his weight from foot to foot with infinite patience and taking care to avoid the creaky parts of his bedroom floor.

Once on the landing, he edged along the wall, almost climbing on the skirting boards to avoid detection. He reached the top of the stairs and lowered himself down the first two steps, hugging the balustrade for support. He brushed aside a tangle of plastic holly and tinsel so he could see through to the open living room door. He’d done this before in an attempt to watch what his parents had told him he couldn’t on TV.

It wasn't the television that had his attention tonight. He wanted to hear what Mummy and Daddy – the nightmare had reverted him to baby names and Robbie was too big for those now – what Mum and Dad were saying.

For a long moment, neither of them said anything.

Robbie's Mum broke the silence.

"It's the same dream, isn't it? After all these years the same dream."

She sounded frightened, and the very idea that there were things in this world that frightened even Mum was enough to turn Robbie's blood to ice.

"Yes, it's the same. I couldn't get a lot of sense out of Robbie, but I got enough. He was even holding himself exactly where…" Patrick's voice faded out. Perhaps he was scared, too. At the very least he sounded confused and Robbie didn't like that. Parents weren't supposed to be scared or confused. They were supposed to make you feel better and always know what to do.

"Jess was the same." She paused before adding, "I never really believed you, you know?"

"What do you mean?"

"Well, it was all so incredible. I didn't think you were lying. Not exactly. I just thought it was, I don't know, a story your parents told you that you heard so often it started to feel true. Something like that."

“My parents never talked about it. Not then. They did what we did tonight. They told us everything was OK, nothing to be scared of and pretended nothing like this had ever happened before.”

“We can’t tell them, can we?” said Joanna.

“No,” said Patrick, “Just because I hate Christmas, I don’t want them to have to.”

Joanna didn’t reply. Again, the silence descended.

Robbie leaned forwards, hating what was he hearing and yet desperate to hear more. What did any of this have to do with Christmas? And then he remembered. The last thing he heard in his dream. *Silent Night;* a Christmas carol.

He was so focused on what was happening downstairs, he was oblivious to what was happening behind him.

He didn’t see the ghostly white figure approach. He didn’t hear the tiny footsteps. He didn’t sense something getting closer and closer.

A hand landed on his shoulder.

Robbie couldn’t help himself. For the third time that night he screamed.

Jess put her hand over his mouth to stifle the noise, but it was too late.

“What are you kids doing out of bed?”

There was no fear in Joanna's voice now. The two children bolted back to their bedrooms.

"Back to bed, you two," shouted Patrick. Robbie was under the covers before he'd finished the sentence. Nightmares were one thing, but two angry parents, that was proper scary. Dreams can't take away your iPads or lock up your Lego.

Robbie closed his eyes tight to demonstrate that he was really trying to go to sleep.

Robbie heard his mother close the living room door, but before it was completely shut he heard her say "Do you think they heard us?"

#

Like every Christmas Eve Robbie could remember, the day passed infinitely slowly. Eventually, the time came. Jess and Robbie were marched upstairs. Jess complained all the way, falling back on her favourite argument - as the oldest she should get to stay up later than her little brother.

Robbie mounted the stairs like he was walking to the electric chair.

"Dad, can we leave the light on tonight?"

"If we do that, Santa might not come."

"Da-ad!" said Robbie, "I'm not 6."

"Sorry," said Patrick, "I tell you what, just this once, you can leave the light on."

Robbie blinked. He started to say "Thank you", but the look in his father's eyes stopped him.

He knows, thought Robbie. He knows what's going to happen.

Robbie heard the church clock and counted the chimes off on his fingers. Midnight. It's Christmas Day. If anything is going to happen, it'll start now.

He glanced around his bedroom. Even with the light on it was full of unfamiliar shapes and shadows. Robbie pulled his Transformers duvet up to his face leaving just his eyes peeping out from within.

Robbie shivered. His curtains began to billow as though blown by a gale. The window was closed. He had just enough time to be grateful that his father had left the light on before the bulb shattered with an echoing pop.

Robbie tried to scream but found that he couldn't. He was close enough to his door to get out of the room in a few steps, but he couldn't move either. The door might as well have been a mile away.

As his eyes became accustomed to the dark Robbie saw that he was no longer alone. Standing in the furthest corner of the room was – what? It was too tall to be a child, but he couldn't make out enough detail to tell if it was a man or a woman. The figure turned slowly until it was facing him.

Still unable to discern any features, Robbie was suddenly sure this was a man. Or had been a man at some point. I'm seeing a ghost, he thought, an actual real ghost. Ghosts are real and I know it and I'm not going to be able to tell anyone because I can't move and I don't think I'm going to get out of this alive.

The ghost took a step towards Robbie. Another step, then another. One more step and he'd be at the foot of Robbie's bed.

As he got closer, Robbie could see more clearly.

It was a man, but a fairly young one. He was wearing a uniform, similar but not identical to the one Robbie saw in his nightmare.

The ghost was pointing something at Robbie – he realised without surprise that it was a revolver. The ghost pulled the trigger over and over again. Nothing happened.

Robbie tried to shout what might have been a warning or might have been a cry for help, but he still could not speak. The ghost stared in horror at his gun and looked back towards Robbie for a split second before he flew backwards, landing on his back out of Robbie's sight.

Robbie found he could move again. He dived not for the door but the end of his bed. He got there just in time to see the ghost fade out of view, bright red blood gushing from a wound in its chest. A few moments later, the ghost was gone and the room was warm.

All that remained was a pool of blood on Robbie's carpet.

He found his voice and screamed as loud as he could. In another room, Jess was screaming, too.

#

Much later, Robbie and Jess sat on Robbie's bed bathed in light from a newly-replaced bulb. After having shared a nightmare the previous evening, they were not surprised that they both had visitations from what they agreed was a ghost. They were much more concerned by what happened next.

"Why did Mum have a torch?" asked Jess. "And how did they get to us so quickly? They must have been…"

"Just outside the door," finished Robbie.

The two siblings stared at each other in silence for a long time.

"They know, don't they?" said Jess.

Robbie nodded.

"But why…?"

Jess didn't finish her question.

Neither of them had an answer.

"So what do we do now?"

#

Robbie spent the rest of the night on the floor of Jess's bedroom. It wasn't comfortable, but he got more sleep there than he would have done alone in his own bed.

For the first time ever, their parents had to wake them on Christmas morning. The distinct aroma of slowly roasting turkey already filled the house. Jess and Robbie did their best to feign enthusiasm about their many gifts, but their interest lay elsewhere.

Christmas Day was a day of tradition in the Carstairs household. After the presents were opened the children would be allowed a couple of hours to play with their many new toys while Mum and Dad busied themselves with Christmas Dinner and preparing for the arrival of the extended family that afternoon. Those two hours offered Robbie and Jess their best chance of putting their plan into action.

"We're going to take our presents to our room," said Jess. Joanna seemed surprised – it usually took several days to get the kids to do that.

The children had other reasons for being upstairs. In addition to their bedrooms, which right now were not particularly welcoming places, it also gave them access to the attic.

Robbie dragged a heavy chair from their parents' room to the landing. Jess stood watch at the top of the stairs.

Once the chair was in place, Jess, who was a little taller than Robbie, clambered first onto the seat, and then, more precariously, to the arms. Robbie held the chair in place as Jess made the tiny jump necessary for her to reach the access hatch and pull down the ladder.

#

Robbie was disappointed by the attic. He'd only seen glimpses of it until now and it had attained a level of magic and wonder in his mind that the reality didn't merit. It was just mouldy boxes, dust and a faint smell of slow decay.

"Do you know which one it is?"

Jess surveyed the room with an air of someone who's suddenly not sure they had a good idea after all. Unlike Robbie, she had been up there before. Which box had Dad stopped her looking at?

Robbie lifted the lid off the nearest box, spluttering slightly at the flurry of dust the movement created. The contents were less interesting than the box – an old hairdryer, three scratched vinyl LPs – this item confused Robbie a little but he was happy to just assume it was something old they didn't need any more, and a calendar from 2002. He became aware that Jess hadn't moved.

"Come on, Jess, which one? We can't be up here long."

“Shhh!” said Jess, not looking at him. “I’ll find it.”

Robbie opened another box.

“Got it!” shouted Jess. Robbie turned to glare at her, “Shhh…”.

“I know,” said Jess, “But look…”

Robbie looked. “It’s just a load of old paper,” he said.

Jess shot him a withering look that seemed to say, “What were you expecting?”. She turned her attention back to her discovery. “This stuff looks old enough and Dad shut me down pretty quickly when I saw it last time. This has to be it.”

“Can you lift it?”

“I think so.”

“Good, then let’s get out of here.”

#

Back in Jess’s room, Robbie grabbed a sheaf of paper but he found it difficult to make any sense of them. Jess, being two years older and a more accomplished reader, did better.

“We’re looking for something from the early 1900s,” she said.

“Why then?” asked Robbie.

“Our dreams. The soldiers. The battlefield. I’ve read about World War One and I’m pretty sure that’s where it’s all from.”

Jess sorted through the various papers, discarding everything that didn’t seem to date back that far. It was a cutting from a newspaper that caused her to stop dead.

“It’s him, isn’t it?” said Jess, the pitch of her voice rising, “It’s him.”

Robbie leaned forward for a closer look. The clipping contained a rough reproduction of an old photograph. The picture was hazy, but then so had been their first look at the person depicted. Robbie felt the colour drain from his face.

“Y-yes. It’s him.”

Jess swallowed hard and started to read the article under the photo.

“Says here this is… Corporal Patrick Carstairs.”

The name brought her to a halt. Patrick Carstairs.

“Well, it’s not Dad, is it?” said Robbie.

Jess laughed. “No, it’s not Dad. It must be his great grandfather or something… Oh. No. Not grandfather.”

“Why not grandfather?”

"Because he died. When he was 19. Maybe he's a great Uncle or something."

"19? Did he… in the War?"

Jess read silently for a few more moments.

"Um. Yes. Sort of. He was executed. He was… shot by a firing squad."

Robbie blinked back a tear, surprised to be moved by the death of a relative he'd never heard of before.

"Why?"

Jess read on. "It doesn't… ah, hang on. Here it is. Shot for 'dishonouring his regiment'. He killed a German soldier during a ceasefire."

"Ceasefire?"

"You know, a truce. They'd agree to stop all the shooting for a time. This was on… of course! Christmas Eve!"

Robbie gave his sister a glare.

"OK, so… in the First World War there was a famous ceasefire. It was Christmas Eve and all the soldiers came out of their – trenches, I think they called them – and sang carols. They even played football."

"And when they were supposed to not be shooting, this Patrick shot –"

"It doesn't actually say he shot him. Just says he killed a German…" Jess tailed off as their eyes met and they both reached the same conclusion.

"That's the dream!" Robbie continued, "That's what we saw. Patrick Carstairs killed the German. That's –"

"Who the ghost is," said Jess. "No wonder he's so cross."

"Why don't we already know all of this?" said Robbie. "Dad must know."

"It's because we don't talk about it," said a new voice. Patrick stood at the door. The children whirled around in a panic, but they could see right away that their father wasn't angry. He looked sad. Desperately sad. Joanna stood behind him looking no happier.

"I think maybe it's time," she said quietly. Patrick looked at her as though he'd never seen her before. He smiled ruefully.

"Yes, I think it is."

#

"Great *Great* Uncle Patrick – Great *Great* Great Uncle Patrick as he is to you – is our family's darkest secret. You already know the worst of it. In the middle of a ceasefire, Christmas 1914, he killed an unarmed German soldier. The shame almost killed his parents and younger brother."

"He wasn't unarmed," said Robbie quietly.

The other stared him so he said it again.

"He wasn't unarmed. The German soldier. He had a gun."

"But it didn't work," said Jess. "It was too muddy."

"Patrick didn't know that," said Robbie. "He just saw a man with a gun trying to kill him."

His father nodded.

"I've seen that, too."

"I know," said Robbie.

Patrick blinked.

"You've had the dreams, haven't you? You've seen the ghost."

"You were waiting on the landing. You had torches," said Jess.

"Yes. I've had the dream. A long time ago."

"At Christmas?" asked Jess, understanding starting to dawn.

"Yes. Christmas 1982. When I was your age, Robbie. And Christmas 1983, And 1984. And 1985. And 1986."

"What happened after that?"

"They just stopped. They always do. Ever since 1914, Carstairs children start having the dreams and the uh, visits, from the Christmas when the youngest reaches eight and they continue until that youngest child is twelve. We've tried moving. We've tried being away from home at Christmas. Nothing works."

"So that's what this ghost is," said Jess. "It's a German soldier who's angry that he was killed. Does he want to hurt us? Does he want revenge?"

"He can't hurt you," said Joanna, a shade too quickly.

"I think that's true," said Patrick.

"But he wants to?" said Jess.

Patrick nodded.

"No," said Robbie. Again, they all turned to look at him.

"He doesn't want to hurt us," said Robbie.

Patrick stared at his youngest child, baffled.

"Don't you see? He's not angry with Patrick. He's angry with himself. He feels bad about what happened."

"Yes!" said Jess, "I think that's it."

Her parents still stared blankly.

"Don't you see?" said Jess, "The German soldier didn't know there was a ceasefire. He'd been injured, who knows how long he was out there? He sees this British soldier and he tries to defend himself. Patrick sees the gun and he does the same. It was a misunderstanding."

"Yes," said Robbie, "That's it."

Joanna was nodding now. "All these years," she said to Patrick, "all this time your family has been hiding their little secret and this –", she swallowed, feeling more than a little silly as she said the word "ghost" – "this ghost wants you to know there's nothing for you to feel ashamed about. Any of you."

Patrick shook his head.

"Do you really …?"

"Think about it, Dad. It makes sense."

"Maybe," said Patrick, "but even if it does, what do we do?"

"It's obvious, isn't it?" said Robbie.

Joanna and Jess were nodding now.

"Not to me," said Patrick.

"Dad," said Jess, "we give the ghost what he wants. All he's ever wanted."

"We forgive him," said Robbie.

"On behalf of our whole family, including all those who went before," agreed Joanna, "we forgive him. Can you do that?"

Patrick closed his eyes. He could feel the weight of generations lifting off his shoulders.

“Yes. I can forgive. I do. I forgive you!” Patrick shouted the last part into the air. An ice-cold wind scythed through the room. Then it was gone.

That night the Carstairs family slept well. And they never had to fear Christmas again.

The Light of the Christmas Star

by Stephen Wade

The last time we saw each other we were in our late teens. We had met originally as kids when my family used to holiday in his part of the country. Not sure what made me track him down, but I did.

Social media, which didn't exist thirty years ago, made it easy. Next to his name a photo of an impressive looking guest house.

I sent him an email letting him know I was due to attend a conference in his neck of the woods in the next few weeks. Just before Christmas. He didn't reply to my email. But a few days later, an unknown number rang on my phone.

"Hello?" I said, with the requisite rise in my voice. But I instinctively knew it was him before he spoke.

"Conor?" he said. "Is that you Conor?"

"Yes," I said, keeping up the formality. "Conor here. Who's this?"

"Hello Mhac," he said, using his native Irish. Mhac is the Irish for son. "It's me."

"Tomas," I said. It's great to hear from you, man."

We spoke for a while, reminiscing about those long ago days when the world almost made sense. When catching frogs near the well on his family's small plot, and riding the poor old hobbled donkey in their fields was all that the world should be. We spoke too about the Christmas holidays we'd spent together, visiting homes in his area, where old people sat around open fires, laughing and telling seasonal ghost stories.

"Did you ever get married yourself?" he said.

"No," I said. "Came close a few times. But the girls always got sense and left me." I laughed. "The story of my life. How about you?"

"I did," he said, and a tone that could have been confusion or mild terror came into his voice as he told me he didn't want to go there right now. "But, listen to me. Do you have a place to stay itself when you're coming down?"

I explained that I usually stayed in a particular hotel. I'd been attending that conference for a few years now.

Typical of the hospitable country folk I remembered as a boy, he wouldn't hear of it. There were very few guests in his home that time of year. And, for the moment, nobody had booked any rooms for December. So there'd be plenty of room for me.

Despite my protestations, he talked me into it. And over the next few weeks, he convinced me too to leave the car at home. The train was far more relaxing. He'd drive in to the city himself and collect me on the evening after the conference.

The evening arrived. A particularly cold one, in the air a suggestion of snow. The streets crowded with Christmas cheer and colourful lights.

As agreed, I waited next to the stone monument memorialising the state visit of one of the United States' most respected presidents. Back in the day when U.S. presidents deserved respect. I was reading the inscription on the tablet when I heard a man's deep voice use my name.

"Tomas," I said, hoping the astonishment I felt at his appearance didn't come across in my voice or my expression.

His large though frail hand enveloped mine. "The light of the Christmas star to you," he said.

"Agus a thabhairt," I said. *And to you.*

"Do you have the Irish now?" he said.

"That's about it," I said.

This put paid to any awkwardness either of us might have been feeling meeting up after so long.

But that awkwardness, for me, was replaced by shock. As outlandishly tall as he was thin, his gaunt face was how it might appear had he been lying in an open coffin for a number of days.

The drive back to his home terrified me. Or, more specifically, his driving did. He tore through the narrow country roads as though he were a Formula One driver. He kept turning to look at me when taking sharp bends while making some point or imitating some character we'd both known from our childhoods.

A moonless night when we pulled in to the front of his house. Tomas switched of his headlights and killed the engine. An instant blackout. Living in the city, I'd forgotten how utterly pitch the night can be without artificial lighting. I stepped from his jeep and felt something cold and wet nuzzle the back of my hand. Too dark to make out anything, I patted the animal and listened to its appreciative panting. Tomas was busy fumbling with his keys and the front door.

"Come in," he said.

"God bless all here," I said half-jokingly, yet with sincerity, as I stepped into the house.

"It's only myself that's in it," he said, as he lit a thick red candle in the hallway.

"But you have a good dog to keep you company anyway," I said, waiting for him to tell me in his own time about where his wife was. And children, if he had any.

"I don't have a dog," he said. "Not anymore."

Something cold slid down the back of my neck, and I felt the hairs on my forearms bunch.

"I'll be back in a moment," he said. "Make yourself at home."

I pushed the front door to behind me. And when I turned about, I saw his flickering shadow disappear around a corner. I followed it into what was the sitting room, which led through a door-less archway into another room, a large kitchen. Through the actual kitchen door, which was slightly open, I heard Tomas coughing in a room down the hallway. And then I heard him speaking in his native Irish, his tone slightly higher than when he spoke in English. And there was a woman's voice, very faint. I backed away into the living room and sat down in an armchair.

Presently, I awoke to realise I'd nodded off. Coming from the kitchen, I heard the clink and clang of cups and cutlery. The hiss of water from a tap.

"Don't be going to any trouble for me, Tomas," I called out.

No reply.

"Tomas," I said, as I pushed myself to my feet and worked my way around a coffee table and into the kitchen. I stopped.

"Oh, excuse me," I said to a small female figure dressed in black standing over the sink. "You must be," I trailed off. "Tomas told me that you were, em. Sorry, I'm Conor." I held out my hand, waiting for her to turn my way.

I watched the weak reflection in the window of the woman's face watching me. But she didn't turn about. My extended hand I let fall back by my side.

Because of the deathly blackness outside, her reflected face might have been on the outside looking in. Somehow this disturbed the hell out of me. An invisible claw raked down my spine. Again I reversed into the living room, excusing myself for intruding as I went.

"Were you calling me?" Tomas said as he opened a door down the hallway out of sight.

On my feet to meet him when he stepped into the room, I reiterated that I didn't want to be putting anyone out. And that I'd eaten on the train journey down.

"Not at all," he said. "Come on inside."

I followed him into the kitchen.

"I see you've put the kettle on," he said. "Good man."

Before I could answer him he was singing my praises on how I'd guessed his favourite mug. He then poured us mugs of tea, grabbed a packet of custard creams, put them on a tray and carried it into the sitting room.

"Sugar?" he said.

"No thanks," I shook my head.

"A healthy man," he said.

I smiled and wrapped my hands around the mug to warm them, while I listened to him list off a myriad of health problems from which he suffered. But in a jokey, self-deprecating way. And as he recounted his different medical conditions, along with accidents he'd had, and the subsequent visits and stays in hospital, he piled turf sods into the open fireplace. Soon the room was filled with a smoky-brown peaty fug, which gave off a smell that complimented Tomas's tales and biographical snippets.

Blind in one eye, he told me, with less than eighty per cent in the other.

But he drove his jeep like a sighted person. Having me on, he was.

No, it was true. "Like playing a fiddle," he said. With this he stood up and took a walking stick from off the wall, where it had been hanging as an ornament.

I admitted that I didn't get it.

"In front of a crowd in a pub. When one of the strings break." He held the blackthorn stick beneath his chin the way you would a violin. "You improvise. Keep playing." He moved an invisible bow across the stick. "That, or you skulk back to your seat."

I nodded, but didn't believe the analogy. He put the walking stick back on the wall and sat back down.

Tomas then reached out and took a pipe off the mantelpiece, which I only noticed then was lined with holly and berries. But the leaves were brown and yellowed, the berries wizened. He then went about cleaning the pipe, before cutting up a cube of tobacco on a small marble slab with a blue penknife. The tobacco flakes he thumbed into the pipe's bowl. I watched as he sucked in a few times while he held a match above the bowl. The flame jerked up and down, and as the tobacco caught and he pulled in and released the blue smoke, a new scent mingled with and then overrode the smell of burning turf. A sweet and uplifting smell redolent of thoughtful and contented old men sitting around a country cottage.

The sound of his voice saying something to me and laughing made me realize I'd nodded off again.

"Don't worry, Mhac," he said. "Did you want to turn in?"

Not wishing to appear ungrateful, I thought it best if I at least stayed up and chatted with him for a while yet. But I did use the excuse of needing to use the bathroom so I could splash some water on my face. As I pushed myself from the armchair, I commented on his wedding photos on the wall. I'd glanced at them earlier without really taking them in.

"At the beginning of the millennium," he said. "We got married in the spring that year."

I recognised his bride in the photos as a younger, more vital version of the woman I had seen in the kitchen.

“Sixteen years,” he said. “We were man and wife for sixteen years.”

I turned about to listen to him.

“This time last year she was in this very room writing Christmas cards.” He laughed fondly. “Oh yes, Alannah. She loved Christmas.” He shook his head and massaged his temples with his fingertips.

“How do you mean she *loved* Christmas?” I said.

“Not long till Christmas morn,” he said. “With the longest night and the shortest day behind us, I lost her. When the first ewes were lambing.” He smiled forlornly. His face darkened for a moment before a forlorn smile relieved his taut facial muscles.

“I’m sorry,” I said, though at that instant I felt more dread than the sympathy I expressed.

“It’s okay,” he said. “But, listen, go on now with you to the toilet.” He directed me to the room he had waiting for me upstairs.

As I left the sitting room and stepped into the hall, I heard the light click off behind me. I twisted about and looked at Tomas’s seated figure in the darkened corner, his gaunt features highlighted by the dying embers in the fire. I made an attempt at a joke, something stupid like I hoped he wasn’t planning on cracking open my skull with the blackthorn stick when I came down. I laughed. He didn’t. He made no reply at all.

When I stepped into the bedroom upstairs, I automatically turned the key in the lock before using the en suite bathroom. But while in the bathroom, I once more heard the sound of voices, a man's and a woman's, coming from downstairs. Wild thoughts and images went through my head: Tomas's story was concocted. He and his wife were one of those rare killer couples. A Freddie and Rosemary West. Brady and Hindley. They lived in a home deep in remote countryside, surrounded by acres of bogland. The perfect place to bury the remains of tortured and dismembered bodies.

My stomach tightened. That's when the voices below grew louder, with Tomas's voice clear and harsh, the woman's high and terrified. The tone suggested she was pleading with him. And then the sound of banging and thumping, as though they were crashing into furniture.

Overriding my own terror, I hurried from the bathroom and unlocked the bedroom door, but it wouldn't open. I pulled and rattled and banged on it, calling out for Tomas to open up. And all the while the roaring, the shouting, the banging continued relentlessly.

My phone. I pulled my phone from my jeans pocket. No signal. And, at that very moment, the sidelights and a bedside lamp went out, leaving me in darkness. I fumbled about for the switch, but it wouldn't work. And the warmth in the room too seemed to be sucked out. In its place an instant plummet in temperature.

“Tomas,” I shouted while hammering my fists on the door. “Let me out of here. Tomas, what the hell’s going on?”

That’s when I heard a scream so terrible, it didn’t sound like it had come from a human larynx. Silence followed, broken only by my retching. When I stopped, I heard what sounded like the front door being opened. Laboured breathing peppered with curses Tomas had taught me when we were kids. And I could picture him struggling with the dead weight of his wife’s lifeless or unconscious body.

Fighting against the dizziness and nausea, I once more pulled and banged on the door. To no avail. Except for the handle, which came off in my hand.

“Jesus Christ,” I said, twisted about and dashed the handle at the window. The crash of broken glass somehow emboldened me. I worked my way across the room, my eyes adjusting now to the darkness, complimented by the bony light of the emerging moon thrown through the skylight and window. Through the window I could make out what appeared to be a figure or figures moving laboriously through the rock-strewn shadows of the rear field.

“Tomas,” I shouted through the broken windowpane.

The figure stopped for a second before moving on.

I attempted to open the window, but like the door, it wouldn’t budge. Without forethought, I raised my leg and pressed the sole of my foot against the broken glass. It gave way easily, the glass shards sliding down the slated roof before falling and shattering on the ground below. Careful to avoid cutting my hand, I whipped a blanket from the bed and threw it across the grill. The dormer window led onto a few feet of roof. I eased my way through the window, the rain drenched roof soaking into my jeans.

With my feet resting on the gutter, which felt quite solid, I prepared to let go of the grill and bend my knees so I could grab the gutter. That's when the gutter gave way beneath my feet, which made me shift one hand and hold tighter. But in doing so, a piece of broken glass in the grill pierced through the blanket and into the palm of my hand. This caused me to let go, giving me time enough to be aware that I was about to hit the ground.

I awoke disoriented. In the sky the moon was gone. In its place a star of molten-gold so stunning it might have been painted by a child.

For how long I'd been out I had no idea. In my head competing pains. A freezing headache and a physical pain, as though I'd been smashed in the back of the head with a baseball bat - or perhaps a walking stick. That reminded me - Tomas. His wife. The argument. The screaming. The window. My fall.

I lay where I was for some time, not sure if my body still worked.

With the paling of the day, and the first weak rays of the winter sun, I finally pushed myself on to an elbow. And from there into a seated position. And then to my feet.

My first attempts to walk caused a stabbing pain to catch me in the lower back. But I persevered, deciding it was probably just a muscular injury. I made my way around the side of the house to the front door. But for a second or two, my eyes refused to believe what was before them. Across the door was a large board - painted white. While the windows were barred up with sheets of corrugated Iron. Likewise painted white. And then there was Tomas's jeep. It sat on concrete blocks. Its wheels missing.

Something exceptionally weird was going on. I reversed back around the side of the house to the rear and in the direction I'd seen Tomas's figure going in the night. But when I saw a couple of sheep grazing in the field I began to doubt myself. Maybe that's what I had seen from the window during the night. Those doubts grew stronger as a large black cow came out from behind a gorsy hill.

"Good morning to you," a strong voice called from a distance.

I almost slipped where I stepped but managed to stay on my feet. I turned about to see a stocky man climbing over a low stone wall. I squinted in an effort to see him more clearly as he walked towards me.

"That's a fine sort of a morning," he said.

I nodded.

“Who is it you’re looking for?” he said.

Deciding to play things cautiously after my experience, I told him I was a childhood friend of Tomas. And that I’d been in the neighbourhood and on impulse had tracked him down. To surprise him.

The man, who was in his sixties, looked me over. I could see the scepticism in his eyes. He pushed the cap back on his forehead and said I looked as though I’d slept outside through the night. And how did I get there? He craned his neck to where only Tomas’s jeep sat on the blocks in the driveway.

I laughed off my appearance, and told him I’d been celebrating with a few friends in the city. A Christmas get-together. And one of them had driven me out to Tomas’s place afterwards. But I didn’t remember too much after that. The drink must have got to me I said.

“Well, tis lucky you woke up to see the day at all,” he said.

“I’m good,” I said. “Soon as I have a hot shower and something to eat, I’ll be flying.”

We shared a laugh together, this stranger and I, before he told me that he had some unfortunate news to tell me. But, first of all, he suggested that I get the damp clothes off my back, take a shower and get a bit of grub inside me. He invited me back to his home to meet his wife. There was no better woman for looking after a man, he said.

Once more I found myself deeply moved by the humanity and generosity of country people. He even offered me a strong arm and shoulder to lean on as he led me down Tomas's drive to where his car was parked on a boreen - a little road.

The man and his wife did just as he had offered. And very soon I was sitting in their kitchen after a hot shower. Wrapped up in some of the man's newest clothing – a pair of dark slacks, a T-shirt and a heavy cardigan. In front of me a large plate of fried eggs, rashers, black and white pudding, cherry tomatoes, mushrooms, baked beans, hash browns, and a steaming, hot mug of tea. I thanked them both profusely and, in truth, could have wept at their genuineness and hospitality. Given the emotional state I was then in.

Having exchanged potted biographies, the conversation came round to Tomas. The man put down his knife and fork and leaned into the table.

"You see," he said, "Tomas's wife took up with an English chap who'd been holidaying here regularly for a few years. An open secret it was. Tomas knew too. But didn't let on."

The man's wife began clearing the plates away. She asked me if I'd have another mug of tea. And a mince pie.

"Yes," I said, passing her my empty plate and mug. "Thank you. That was delicious."

The man went on. "Tomas's wife began taking short trips to England during the year. To visit her sister, she told everyone. Then one day she disappeared and never returned."

About my now full stomach there seemed to tighten an invisible belt. The man clearly saw the change in my countenance while he recounted how everyone accepted that Tomas's wife had left for England for good to be with the Englishman.

"Are you okay, Sir?" he said.

"Yes," I said. "Well, no, just a little, you know? I think I ate too fast. That's all. But, please, go on. What happened to Tomas?"

What this man told me next was something for which I wasn't prepared. And it's something that will stay with me always.

Christmas Eve, it was, he told me. The same day Tomas's wife was last seen when she went to the local post office. The day she posted a letter to Tomas outlining her reasons for leaving him. A letter he would never receive. For that very night Tomas walked himself through the fields he had walked thousands of times. Up to his barn he went, where he took from the wall a blue rope he sometimes fashioned into a halter for his bay mare. This time he fashioned one end into a hang-noose.

As his closest neighbour, the man recalled how it was he who had first noticed Tomas's larger livestock behaving in an unusual manner that fateful day, as he put it. On Christmas morning.

"A bit jittery they were," he said. "The milking cow clearly needed to be milked. While the bay mare, a usually quiet animal, whinnied and nickered in the field next to the open barn door."

Shaking his head, I could see and feel his horror as he described finding Tomas's lifeless body swinging from a wooden beam in the barn.

When the man had finished his story about Tomas, it was my turn to tell him mine. Hesitant though I was for fear of him thinking me some kind of crackpot, he encouraged me with nods of affirmation and an expression that not for one second doubted the legitimacy of my tale.

"Right," he said when I was through. He closed his eyes and stroked his stubbly chin with smoke-stained fingers. "This changes everything."

Later that morning we were back on Tomas's land with police officials, one of them a member of the aqua unit. Within an hour the skeletal remains of Tomas's wife were recovered from the well. The original cold and clinical verdict that Tomas had died through misadventure would, in time, be updated to murder-suicide.

"The light of the Christmas star to you," the man said while shaking my hand when he dropped me off in the square where I'd met Tomas the night before.

That's when I finally came undone.

Just Your Imagination

by Lizzy Bayly

(Children's Highly Commended)

I watched as my deceased cousin's wife ascended to the pulpit. Her face was stony, cold and beneath it I was sure emotion must be roiling, however it wasn't obvious and I couldn't help but wonder if she was bothered about it at all. But I settled myself and as my cousin-in-law opened her mouth, I prepared myself for what she was about to say.

She didn't recount the happy times she spent with him. She didn't start by telling us how lucky she was to be married to him. All she said was:

"What you're about to hear will not be something you've ever heard before." And then she began. "We were married in the south-east of England, in Dover, as I'm sure you all know as relatives of Edmund. We were both born from not very well-off families, so even our combined money couldn't get us abroad for our honeymoon. This led us to visit Edmund's parents in Scotland, as it didn't cost much money, it was a change of scene, and we could stay at my new parents-in-law's house. We loved going for walks in the countryside also, so it seemed like the perfect place.

“Three days into the honeymoon, we went for a nice walk half an hour away from Edmund’s parents’ house. It was on a marsh and we had planned to be out for the whole day, arriving back at around 7 o’clock, and we decided to have lunch at a tavern on the middle of the marsh. There, we had a meagre lunch, as much as we could afford, and Edmund had a pint of beer.

“I thought there must’ve been something in the beer, as only an hour later as we continued our walk, he doubled over and started coughing violently. I tended to him and eventually I decided that I must at least get him back to the tavern, for he would catch his death in the cold and we wouldn’t be able to get him back to his parents’ house.

“It took us over 2 hours, but I hauled him into the tavern and asked for a room, for they had some for travellers around the area. It was most of the rest of our gold, but we did it anyway. We stayed overnight and I didn’t get much sleep as Edmund was so ill: coughing sickly, racked with violent shivers and occasionally throwing up. I couldn’t think of any illness that matched the description.

“There was nothing I could do, so I thought I had better try to get some sleep. I slept fitfully, tossing and turning, but when I woke up, Edmund was sleeping peacefully and he no longer looked pale. I wondered if it had all just been a bad dream.

“I knew Edmund’s parents must have been worrying about where we were, so we decided to walk back that day as

Edmund was feeling cheerful and much better. It took us only a few hours and I explained the whole incident to my mother-and-father-in-law. They shrugged it all off and said I must've imagined it, and that made me feel a bit stupid.

"Our honeymoon finished successfully and I decided that I must've imagined it. There was no other explanation. We returned home to Dover and settled into our little cottage by the sea. Edmund began his job and we were happy.

"Then one day about a week and a half after our honeymoon, I woke up in the morning to see the other side of our bed empty and realised it hadn't been slept in. I wrapped myself in my threadbare dressing gown, rushed downstairs and searched the entire house, finding nothing. By this time, I was very worried. I didn't bother to get dressed when I ran out of the cottage and spied a figure in the distance.

"I stumbled hurriedly over to the shape, hoping it was him and it was. I was so relieved, I started blabbering to him about how worried I was. He didn't reply. He didn't even look at me. His gaze was fixed on the sea and the clouds. I shook his shoulder and begged him to look at me and he finally obliged.

"But his eyes bore into me and they were black and soulless – there was nothing human in them. For a moment, I thought he was going to throw me off the cliff. But then the moment passed and his eyes returned to a fresh blue and he hugged me and told me there was nothing to worry about. I put it down to my imagination again.

"However, progressively over the next few weeks, he grew nastier and nastier to me. He seemed to speak to me less and every night I found his bed unslept in and his figure staring out at the sea from the cliffs. I grew unhappy and told him so one night when I decided that things needed to change. He quickly grew angry and he snarled at me, gripping my shoulders so tightly that there were bruises and claw marks in them for days.

"I tried running away, but he caught me every time and beat me, every time worse and worse. Once, he broke my arm and wouldn't allow a doctor into the house to treat me, so he bought medical supplies and put it in a sling. I spent weeks in bed, too weak to try to leave. After a long time, Edmund managed to fix my arm and it healed. I recovered, able to try to run away for the first time in two months.

"So I did. No matter what, I knew I had to get out of that house and away from him. I got out the front door and ran as fast as I could across the clifftops. It wasn't long before a figure started getting closer and closer behind me. I changed direction, making a beeline for the cliff edge. I thought that even if I couldn't get away, I could by throwing myself off the side. But he caught me just as I reached it.

"He gripped my shoulder tightly and I thrashed, trying to drag myself away. He was too strong. But I had grown stronger too. Something changed within him and his eyes went black and fear grew in me for I knew that look. I struggled harder, but Edmund had changed tactics and he went for my neck, pressing hard. I knew he was trying to kill me. I stumbled backwards and brought my hands up to clench his wrists.

"Eventually, short of breath, I managed to pull them free and with adrenaline coursing through me, I shoved him away from me and over the cliff. I will never forget the look on his face as he fell. His eyes became blue again and they widened. His calloused, dirty hands reached up to me, he called my name and I knew it was my Edmund – the Edmund I had known. I regretted every second of it. I forgot what he'd done to me. I just wanted my husband back.

"But it was too late. Edmund's body hit the rocks far below with a sickening thwack and his face went cold. I was about to turn away – run away before anyone saw what I had done, when a thick pale cloud rose from his open mouth. It sped away from his body and headed straight for me. I staggered back a few paces, staring in wonder, for it had a face.

"Soulless black eyes dripped tears down grey, grimy cheeks leading to the mouth below that was full of sharp teeth. From its canine-like-teeth, gore hung – but there was something in it. Pictures of Edmund when he was happy.

Him smiling on our first date, when he first met me, laughing with me and how he looked when he slipped my wedding ring onto my finger.

"The creature left me with a realisation. On the marsh that fateful day in our honeymoon, the ghost had entered Edmund. It had slowly been feeding off him, filling his soul with more of the ghost's character every day. It was why my husband had grown nastier and nastier – why he ignored me more and had that glint in his eye that terrified me.

"You may believe me. Or you may not. But if I go to prison for what I've done, that is what I deserve and I will not struggle. I have seen enough in my lifetime."

My cousin's wife descended from the stage, tears running down her smooth cheeks. I was speechless – the whole church was quiet. I didn't believe her of course, but it was a chilling ghost story that sent a shiver down my spine. There was only one other strange thing that happened that day.

After the funeral had finished, I went to the toilet and I heard a strange laughing coming from the women's bathroom. Curious, I slowly pushed open the door. It made no creak, so the person in the bathroom didn't hear me. I peered in and what I saw was something I'd never forget.

Edmund's widow was standing facing the window and tears still soaked her grimy grey skin, her eyes were black and as she laughed, thousands of sharp teeth could be seen.

I shook it off, knowing I was still immersed in the woman's ghost story. Of course it wasn't real. My imagination was tricking me. Imaginations can do that, you know.

Treworgey's Maid

by Ellen Morrison

(2nd Place)

"Fancy taking a break from un-packing and coming for a stroll through Treworgey Woods?" Asked John as he came into the living room.

Brionne was bending over an open cardboard box, emptying out the contents. Standing up, she pushed her mop of frizzy brown curls away from her face and looked at him.

"Treworgey Woods?" she asked.

"You know, we passed it when we drove in to the village yesterday. It might be an ideal place for Mum to take the dog when she comes." He went to the hall and took his coat off the hook. "Fancy coming with me?"

"Umm, well I'd like to at least get the living room unpacked tonight. You go ahead."

John was quite happy to leave Brionne setting up their new home. She would manage to make the place look far homelier and cosy without him. He pulled into the car park of the woods and headed out along the footpath.

Sunbeams streamed through the trees, illuminating the woodland floor. The bed of pine needles beneath his feet gave way slightly with each step. It was so still and quiet that John felt almost has if he were trespassing, and he found himself practically tip toeing in fear of breaking the peaceful silence.

As he carried on along the path, he came to a large grassy clearing. In the centre stood a large statue of a girl. John walked up to it and looked up, quite taken aback. She was in long skirts carrying a bucket, with a bonnet on her head and hair spilling out from under it. She had been captured mid stride, with an animal by her feet that was somewhat weathered.Was it a goose? It reminded John of the top of a sweet tin his Grandmother used to have. As he looked up at her face, somehow, he felt a sort of connection to her, as if an actual person was looking out of those stone eyes. He looked about, to see if there was a plaque or information board of any sort; something that would give him an idea of who she was, and why her statue had been placed here. There was nothing. He looked up at her one last time before picking the path back up on the other side of the clearing.

Just down the path he noticed a deer hide in amongst the trees. He quite fancied a spot of deer stalking, but he could hear a dog barking deeper inside the woods, breaking the natural peace. He smiled to himself; with dog walkers frequenting the area, there was no chance of spotting any wildlife in the day time. He would have to come down here when there was no one else about. Perhaps at dusk one day.

#

"I'm starving." John declared as he stepped in through the door an hour later. "Shall I rustle up something for dinner?"

Brionne stood up, resting her hands on her hips. "Um, you could try, but we haven't even started unpacking the kitchen yet. I thought we might try out the pub? We could introduce ourselves to the locals."

They stepped in through the door of the village pub, to a welcoming warmth emanating from a large open fire, and comforting chatter. A young girl was behind the bar. She beamed widely at them, "Hello, what can I get you?" They ordered the drinks and asked for a menu.

A man sat at the end of the bar looking like he had stopped off on his way home from work. He was in scruffy clothes and boots, that were covered in paint splashes. He had a pint mug, rather than a glass, with a name that John couldn't quite read, etched on it. The man offered a friendly smile, and broke into conversation.

"Lovely Evening."

"Beautiful" offered Brionne.

John smiled in agreement and began to look at the menu.

The man continued to engage them. "Are you the couple who have just bought The Gables?"

"Yes I'm Brionne, and this is my husband John." She extended her hand.

The man leaned forward and took it "I'm Derek. I fitted your Kitchen before the house went on the market."

John smiled. "Great workmanship. The Kitchen was one of the main selling points for us."

Just then there was a shout from the entrance,

"Oy, Dezza! I hope you've got mine in?" Another man, in similar clothes walked over to them.

Derek turned to the girl at the bar "Pour a pint for Terry would you?" The girl began to pour Terry a Pint in another, named mug.

Derek gestured to John and Brionne, "These are the guys who have just moved in to The Gables."

Terry turned and smiled at them. "It's a great place. Kitchen could do with a bit of work though. I don't know what cowboy they had in there, but they left it in a right state didn't they?" He winked mischievously.

Brionne cut him off at the pass. "Derek has already explained that the Kitchen is one of his." She never had been interested in boys bantering and quickly steered the conversation elsewhere; "Unfortunately we haven't had a chance to test drive it yet as all our cooking utensils are still in boxes, which is why we've popped in here. What can you recommend?"

Derek shrugged. "I always go for Treworgey's Revenge."

Brionne scanned the menu for it, "16 ounce Rump Steak!" she exclaimed "I don't think I've built up that big of an appetite. Why's it called Treworgey's Revenge?"

"Lord Treworgey, used to own half the village" piped in Terry. "He fell in love with his dairy maid, Jennifer and was going to marry her despite her being his servant, but she got trampled by one of her cows."

"Best form of revenge isn't it? Not only to kill the cow, but to eat it as well!" interjected Derek with a menacing smile.

Brionne gave a look of disapproval "Hmm, I don't think I fancy steak tonight, after that thought thank you."

"Is that a statue of Jennifer in the clearing down in the woods then? I was down there today, but there was no information on the plinth." John thought he'd asked a simple enough question, but it was met with stony silence.

Derek shifted uneasily on his stool, and Terry shuffled his feet slightly. "Yeah, that's her" Derek responded eventually, "it's been a long time since I've been down there though. I steer well clear of the woods, and if you take my advice, you would to."

John looked from Derek to Terry and back again. "Steer clear of it? It's not private is it? I thought it was Forestry Commission. It looks like an excellent dog walking facility."

"It may have Forestry Commission signs on the gate, but it's her that owns it." said Derek, a little mysteriously.

"Her?" said John

"Jennifer" said Terry, looking at Brionne, obviously waiting for some kind of reaction.

Brionne looked at the two men, and gave a nervous, yet slightly patronising laugh. "Are we listening to ghost stories now then?"

Terry's face looked teasing. There was a slight smile on his lips, and a twinkle in his eye. Derek's face on the other hand told a different story. There was no laughter there, and his eyes if anything, showed a hint of fear.

"Terry may give you the impression he's a cynic like all you newcomers, but just like me and anybody else who's local, when he drives in to town, he goes via Dunhaven, rather than through Treworgey woods. The number of cars that have come a cropper on an apparently clear section of road speaks for itself."

"Car crashes?" John looked at the two men "caused by a Dairy Maid?"

Terry leaned in conspiratorially. "There have been five accidents that I can think of immediately, two of which were fatal. The drivers of the other three all spoke of seeing a young lady dressed in white who was stood in the middle of the road." He left a long, dramatic pause, and when no one interrupted him, he continued. "Of the three drivers who lived, two said they swerved to avoid her, ending up in the ditch. When they got out of the car to see if the girl was ok, she was nowhere to be seen."

John couldn't help but smirk. "And what of the third one?"

Derek looked him straight in the eye. "That was my brother, and I was his passenger." There was an awkward silence for a moment before he continued. "It's getting on for 20 years ago now. I was a youngster, but I remember it as if it were yesterday. It was close to dark, and my brother Tim was taking me on his first outing after passing his driving test. We headed out of the village and down towards the woods. She came out of nowhere. This girl dressed in white from head to toe. She had no shoes on her feet, and a little bonnet on her head. She just stood in the middle of the road looking straight at us, with her hand held up as if telling us to stop. Tim had no time at all, especially being a new driver. He ploughed straight into her. There was an almighty bang, and a crunching, and the squeal of Tim's brakes. We both lurched forward and then back in our seats. Tim was knocked unconscious for a few moments. I thought he was dead at first." Derek looked at the floor, reliving the memory and shook his head before continuing. "As he came to, he turned to me and said I hit her, didn't I? Go to her!"

Derek looked at his audience "Well, I crept out of the car, afraid of what I might see. I inched around the car's bonnet, which was all bent and mangled, but there was nothing there. She had gone."

John snorted shortly, convinced they were spinning a yarn for the newcomers, but an involuntary shiver tingled down his spine none the less. "What, there was damage to the car, but no person?"

Derek nodded sullenly. "There was even blood on the windscreen. We looked all around. We couldn't believe it. We looked under the car, round the back of it, in the hedge on either side of the road. Nothing. We left the car where it was and ran back home to our folks. Tim was a jibbering wreck by the time we got there. We told our folks we'd hit someone, but we couldn't find them. The whole area was searched, by half the village and the police, but she was never found." He looked at John, his eyes no longer having a look of fear, but something more like anger. "Now, anybody that says there's no such thing as ghosts, simply hasn't seen one. She's down there now, guarding those woods, and you won't see me down there as long as I live."

#

As John headed out towards the woods the following evening, determined not to let local tales disrupt his plans, he couldn't help thinking about Derek's story the night before. The men were right, it really was a clear, straight piece of road. There was a bank on either side with nothing but woodland behind. The road surface was smooth, and although a back road, it wasn't single track; two cars going in either direction could pass easily. Why on earth had so many cars ended up in the ditch?

He pulled into the car park, and dutifully phoned Brionne to let her know he was there. She hadn't been at all happy that he was going to the woods after the conversation in the pub and had promised to check in with her when he arrived and when he was leaving. He reckoned he had about two hours of light left, but in order to appease her, he decided only to stay for one. He made his way quietly up to the hide and sat there with his binoculars hoping that despite his short stay he might be lucky to spot a deer.

From the hide, he had a perfect view of the clearing. The dappled evening light made it look quite magical. All he could hear was leaves rustling in the breeze. No dog walkers today. He settled himself down and waited quietly. Just before his hour was up, a squirrel quietly hopped across the grass and sat by the statue plinth. He picked up his binoculars, but found himself, not looking at the squirrel, but noticing that the plinth did have an inscription on it after all. It was more clearly visible from a distance. 'Here lies Jennifer Cotterell' So it wasn't a statue, it was a gravestone. He thought about Derek saying how she owned the woods. He suddenly felt very uneasy. He chided himself for being spooked by silly ghost stories, but still decided it was time he headed for the carpark. The light had faded more than he expected. Signs on the gate on his way in had said that the car park was locked at night. He hoped he wasn't too late. Just as he got to the car he could see a scruffy looking man waiting by the entrance with a big chain and padlock.

"Just in the nick of time young man, I was about to lock you in!" Far from seeming friendly, he sounded rather gruff.

"Sorry" offered John.

"You will be if you're not careful! It's not advisable for folk to be around this area after dark!"

John was getting tired of local superstition, and he certainly didn't want to hear about the dairy maid again. He cut short any niceties, said he would come earlier in the day next time, got in the car and pulled swiftly out of the carpark.

He really wasn't paying attention as he accelerated out onto the road towards home. He was cross and flustered and fiddling with the radio controls when suddenly in front of him on the road there was a flash of white. He couldn't believe his eyes: There was a woman standing in the middle of the road. The air went icy cold, and knowing the stories, he checked there were no other cars or pedestrians in sight, pulled to a complete halt, and put his hazard warning lights on. The woman was wearing a bonnet. Her thick, curly hair was tied up, but more than a few stray strands framed her face and neck. She was in a long white, cotton dress, and sure enough her feet were bare. To his horror she raised a hand up in front of him as if telling him to stop. She looked directly at him and gave a friendly smile before turning her head and looking up at the bank. He followed her gaze. Over the bank leapt a fully grown stag. It jumped onto the road, inches from the car's bonnet. It was magnificent, with a sleek brown coat and fully grown rack of antlers. John could see its breath in the beam of the car head lights as it let out a loud guttural call, before leaping in one swift movement over the bank on the other side of the road.

The woman smiled widely, beckoned John to start moving forward again, and then quickly faded away to nothing. John sat for a few moments in the darkness, his hazard lights still blinking through the silence. Finally, it all became clear. The dairy maid wasn't causing accidents, she was trying to prevent others from a similar fate to her. If he had been just a few inches further up the road, that Stag would have landed right on top of the car, and he would have been just another statistic on this seemingly clear road. With a shaking hand he picked up his phone and called Brionne.

"Brionne?"

Brionne could hear the anxiety in John's voice. "John, are you ok?"

"I'm fine." He let out a deep sigh. "I've seen my Stag, and I've seen Jennifer. Now I'm on my way home."